Falling

FOR THE

Playboy

USA TODAY BESTSELLING AUTHOR

KENNEDY FOX

Kennedy
Fox

Copyright © 2018 Kennedy Fox
www.kennedyfoxbooks.com

Falling for the Playboy
Bedtime Reads, #2

Cover Photo by FuriousFotog
Cover Model: Chase Ketron
Cover design by Outlined with Love Designs
Copy Editor: Mitzi Carroll
Proofreader: Jenny Sims | Editing 4 Indies

WELCOME TO KENNEDY FOX BEDTIME READS!

Steamy love stories you can read in one sitting! After everyone goes to bed for the night, snuggle up with a Kennedy Fox Bedtime Read! These are full-length standalone novels that are filled with humor, witty banter, blistering heat, and are faster-paced, but still have everything you love about a Kennedy Fox book!

"You touch me and it's almost like we knew,
that there will be history between us two."

"There's No Way"
-Lauv feat. Julia Michaels

CHAPTER ONE

OLIVIA

OH GOD. Oh God. *Oh God.*

Panting. Heavy breathing. Toes curling.

Yessssss.

My teeth sink into my bottom lip as a wave of pleasure hits my core, and then...

The piercing sound of my alarm bellows out, and my body shoots straight up in a panic to turn it off. I look and see it's six a.m.

Ugh.

That's the most action I've had in a year, and it was all a damn dream.

I stretch and slide out of bed, mentally going over my to-do list for the day. Walking to my kitchenette, I grab my mug of coffee that's ready to go. I always program my Keurig the night before, so all I have to do is add creamer in the morning.

As I walk toward the bathroom, I blow into my cup and take a small sip. Just as I check my phone, I see Rachel has already left three messages.

Rachel: I need you here by 8 today.

Rachel: Make that 7. Coffee extra hot.

Rachel: Please.

I roll my eyes at her last text, knowing it probably pained her to use that word. Author Rachel Meadows is a #1 *New York Times* Bestselling Author who has hit the list more times than I can count and is known for being socially awkward and blunt. She's in her midforties, and although she writes about romance, she doesn't have a love life because she eats, sleeps, and breathes writing. She's the very definition of a workaholic, which is why *I* work sixty-hour weeks. I maintain her life so she can focus all her energy on her work.

Perhaps if she did have friends nearby or went out with a man once in a blue moon, she wouldn't be so damn uptight 24/7. However, most people could probably say the same thing about me, which is one reason Rachel and I work so well together. Well, that, and I have the tolerance and patience of a saint.

My previous author client, Vada Collins, found her happily ever after and moved to the East Coast, which is how I ended up working for Rachel. Her assistant quit, leaving her in a major bind, and I needed a new job stat. The cost of living in Chicago is too expensive to stay unemployed for long.

So when Rachel Meadows called me back for a second interview, I prayed to the gods for good voodoo because it was the only local job opportunity available at that time. Now, after a year of working for Rachel, I know nearly everything there is to know about her and cater to her every need.

For example, when she says to arrive at seven with extra hot coffee, that's code for come fifteen minutes early and have a protein shake ready to go. Which means I have exactly forty-five minutes to shower, get dressed, stop at the Starbucks half a mile from her apartment, and read through her emails so I can brief her while she sucks down her blended meal.

Or when she's four days away from her cycle, I know to stock up on Andes Mints and red wine. She has two microwavable rice bags that I rotate out, so she always has a hot one ready for her lower back when she needs to lie down after sitting for too long. Though, if she's on a major dead-line, she'll lie in bed with a heating pad and dictate her words to me so she can work through the cramps.

This morning, I woke up early so I wouldn't have to rush, but now I'll be taking a five-minute shower—cold—since I don't have time to wait for the water to warm. All thanks to Rachel deciding at the last minute that I need to arrive an hour early.

I manage to finish my first cup of coffee in the shower, so while my hair is air-drying, I take a few seconds to dab concealer on the bags under my eyes. I'm a workaholic just like Rachel, except I run marathons around her while she carefully crafts her words for thousands of readers. Once I'm dressed in a pencil skirt and tuck in my blouse, I slide on my Chucks, grab my oversized bag with everything I'll need for the day, and rush out the door.

My Uber arrives as soon as I jog down my apartment building stairs. I fly into the back seat, asking him to step on it. He understands my urgency and guns it down the road. I quickly read over Rachel's emails on my phone until we drive up to the Starbucks closest to her place. Since I ordered ahead on the mobile app, I won't have to wait in line, but I'll still be rushing to Rachel's at this rate.

As I hurry inside to grab the coffees, I check my phone and realize I have less than five minutes to get there. We're only half a mile away, but we're on a one-way street, and her building is behind us. Which means instead of having my driver drop me off at her door, I'll have to jog there.

After letting the driver know my plans, I secure my bag over my shoulder and start running down the block. I wear Chucks for this very reason. Running in heels would result in a broken ankle or blisters for days, and I don't have time for that.

"Excuse me, sorry." Holding our cups tightly in my grip, I maneuver my arms up and over my head while I weave in and out of the crowd walking toward me. Glaring because I'm on the wrong side of the sidewalk, they aren't moving out of my way, but I ignore them and push through. For someone as isolated as Rachel, she lives on one of the busiest streets in downtown Chicago. Even though it's convenient when she needs a coffee break or sends me on a random errand, it's hell to get through.

I make it to her apartment building and am greeted by one of the doormen. They all know me by name and often crack jokes about how they aren't even sure a woman lives in the apartment I work in every day.

"Good morning, Sam," I say as I sprint through the lobby. The elevator doors are already open and set to the tenth floor for me. H nods and gives me a small smile. "Thank you! You're amazing!" I call out right just before the doors close.

Sam Evans is in his late fifties, and within my first couple of weeks of working for Rachel, he memorized my work schedule and how many times I come and go throughout the day. Rachel sends me for bagels often, and as soon as I get them for her, she'll decide she wants a smoothie too. Of course, she couldn't have told me that at the same time so I didn't have to run out twice, but that'd be way too convenient for Rachel Meadows. Sam notices these patterns and has picked up on them over the past year. He always makes sure the elevator doors are open and waiting for me every morning, even when I'm early. He's a good man.

I juggle the coffee cups between my elbow and side boob so I can grab the keys from my bag and have them ready to go as soon as I make it to her apartment. Quietly, I open her door and step inside, making sure to shut it with little to no sound at all.

Setting the cups down on the table, I reach into my bag for my ankle wedge booties that cost me a month and a half's worth of rent and change out of my Chucks. They're one of the most expensive things I own, but comfort costs money. If I want to be taken seriously in this business, Chucks won't cut it. Rachel might be a homebody and live in the same clothes for three days in a row, but she expects professionalism from me at all times.

I shove my Chucks inside my bag and reach for the stash of doggie treats I keep in there. Rachel has a dog who absolutely hates me, and as soon as I walk inside, she nearly gnaws on my ankles to let me know I'm not welcome in her home. Angel—ironically named considering she's the mini version of the devil—is a Toy Poodle, and although she's fluffy and has cute pink bows in her hair, she's a predator, and I'm her prey.

5

Angel trots in with the worst doggy stink eye I've ever seen. She lowers her front legs and sticks her ass up in the air as she releases the most pathetic growl. She still hasn't figured out she's only ten pounds, and half of that is from fur alone. I wouldn't hate her so much if she'd give me a chance, but after months of trying to get on her good side, she rewarded me with a nasty bite, so I gave up.

"Oh, I'm shakin' in my boots now. I might even pee myself." I glare at her and toss her a treat. "Hope you aren't allergic to rat poison."

Before I walk into Rachel's office, I put some vegan protein powder in the mixer, along with a banana. I have a feeling she's not going to want it immediately, so I don't add the ice or soy milk. Grabbing our coffees, I manage to walk to Rachel's office without Angel chasing me. I place hers down on her desk without a word and walk to my little desk in the corner. Once my coffee cup is in place, I set my bag down and dig out my laptop, then start it up.

"I'll take my protein shake in twenty," she informs me without a hello or even a thank you.

"Of course." I smile, feeling as if I can finally read her mind. As soon as my laptop turns on, I grab my book and place it on my desk. The *Bible* as I've coined the very large notebook planner has everything about Rachel to success-fully be her personal assistant and to keep her happy. Every detail from her personal life and professional work life is included—schedules, deadlines, likes and dislikes—anything that helps me help her. Reaching for my coffee, I take a sip and relish in the hot liquid.

"Olivia."

"Yes?" I briefly look up from my cup like a deer in headlights.

"I need you to organize my schedule and plans for my upcoming tour. I have that book signing coming up in Dallas, and if I'm going to be traveling, I want other events to attend during that time before I hunker down and start writing the next one. Book two more city stops with three events—or more—at each. A meet and greet, after party, or whatever. Schedule some dinner meetings with bloggers or my PR firm. Just keep me busy. I don't want to be gone too long, so it needs to be within a two-week period of the first signing."

I nearly spit out my coffee as I put it back down on my desk and scramble for my pen. As she continues to ramble, I jot notes down in the "Rachel bible," knowing she won't repeat herself even if I ask. The book signing is three months away, which doesn't give me much time to plan the rest. I'd already booked her flight and hotel for that event, but now I'll have to reschedule her flight and book additional accommodations to meet her requests.

"Any particular cities you have in mind?" I ask, my pen still flying over the paper.

"That's for you to decide. My readers are everywhere," she replies. "You'll also need to get in touch with the cover model for the Bayshore Coast series and let him know about the added travel dates for the other events."

"Of course," I say, rolling my eyes when I know she's not looking. Her cover model for that series is none other than the arrogant playboy, Maverick Kingston.

"He doesn't fly, so you'll have to drive with him and make sure—"

"What?" I blurt out louder than I mean to. This is the first time she's ever mentioned that to me. How was he planning to make it to Dallas in the first place?

I look up to see if she's serious. "Maverick doesn't do

planes, so you'll have to fly to LA where he lives, then drive with him to each city. I'm paying him good money for his public appearances, and I expect him to be at every event—on time and on his best behavior."

"So, you want me to babysit him?" I pinch my brows together, reading between the lines.

"I want you to make sure my investment doesn't get out of control," she clarifies. "My readers are nuts about him, and they'd die for a chance to meet him, so I need you to make sure he gets to where he needs to be on time." She pins me with her eyes as if to dare me to protest. "Will that be a problem for you?"

Yes. "No, not at all."

"Excellent. I'll be flying to each event, and since you'll be driving, keep that in mind when you make plans to give yourselves enough time to travel."

That means I'll need to book a rental car, hotels while we road trip, additional flights to two other cities, and the event spaces. All within ninety days from now. *No pressure.*

Her book signing in Dallas has been planned for over a year, and now she decides to add this to her schedule? It's not like her, but not entirely out of character either. Rachel's impulsive most of the time. One minute, she wants a turkey and bacon sub, and the next, she's a vegetarian, but this is somewhat extreme and random.

"Okay, got it." I finish my notes and start thinking of cities that can realistically be driven to from Dallas. I don't have much time to nail this all down. If she wants to do two more signings with other events in each city, I'll need to call bookstores, her publisher, get the tickets organized, and start marketing for them pronto.

"Oh, and Olivia?"

I look at her, almost scared for what else she has for me. "Yes?"

"I have a strict no fraternizing policy among my employees. I hope that won't be a problem."

I snort, covering my mouth once I realize the noise was audible. She gives me a disapproving look, but I can't help it. That she even felt the need to add that bit makes me want to burst out laughing. "Trust me. That won't even be an issue."

CHAPTER TWO

MAVERICK

SNAP. Snap. Snap.

"Okay, now let's get a few shots of you standing shirtless in front of the skyline," Katie says, glancing out the window at the cloudless Los Angeles sky. It's late afternoon, so the sun is casting a warm glow through the hotel room. It's the perfect time of day for a shoot. As a newish photographer, she's still trying to build her portfolio, and I owed my friend Jacob a favor, which means allowing his little sister to take pictures of me. She's in her early twenties and cute in a girl-next-door kind of way with a short blond bob. Her lips are bright pink, and her black pants are so tight they look painted on. As I slowly undo each button of my dress shirt, I can tell she's growing more nervous and flushed.

I sometimes have that effect on women. *Well, maybe always.*

I look up at her and give her a smirk, which only causes her to blush. "What are you doin' after this?" I ask.

She shakes her head, watching me with a hesitant smile. "Nothing, really."

"Want to grab some food?" I don't typically hang out with professionals after a job, but she's not actually paying me, so I don't see any harm in it, other than her being my friend's sister.

"Umm..." She nervously shifts on her feet, and I let out a small laugh.

"You want me over here?" I ask, noticing the slight tremble of her hands, so I try to change the subject. It's cute that she's nervous.

She nods. I get into position, tucking my hands into my pockets, and she instantly hides behind the lens. Considering I've been modeling since I was sixteen and have a good decade under my belt, I know my marks, how to look at the camera, and how to position my body, making it pretty easy for photographers to get their money shot. My portfolio includes high paying gigs in a few fitness and fashion magazines and cover model for the *New York Times* bestselling romance series by the award-winning author Rachel Meadows. Recently, I filled my schedule until the end of the year for fitness shoots and even signed contracts, but right now, as far as book covers go, I'm exclusive to Rachel. The advance I was given not to be on other romance book covers was well worth it. Ninety days after her last book is released, my exclusivity ends. I'm living the dream, but I'm still waiting for my breakout moment when agents are fighting over me and six-figure deals are being made. I know it'll happen.

I undo the button and lower the zipper as I move my pants farther down my body, showing the V I've worked so hard to perfect and throw my shirt to the ground. I leave the tie around my neck. Katie gulps—loudly—but continues to take pictures like she's a paparazzi.

"Do you want to get on the bed?" she asks, nervously.

"Only if you join me."

Her eyes go wide.

"I'm kidding," I reassure before I go to the bed. Katie moves to different positions in the room, asks me to change poses, and after an hour of taking photos, she's finally done. I button my pants and pick up my shirt as she scrolls through the photos she's taken.

"So, get some good ones?" I ask, carefully buttoning up my shirt.

"Yeah, totally did. Oh, can I get you to sign this release? If I sell any of these photos, I'll make sure to give you a cut."

"It's not a big deal." I give her a wink. "I owed your brother big time for recommending me for a job. The only thing is, these photos can't be used in the publishing media as far as e-books and paperbacks until my exclusivity expires."

"Oh, I know. My brother told me you weren't going to be released for that stuff until after summer. He repeated himself about thirty times." She chuckles. "So, about dinner..." She hesitates, turning off her camera and kneeling to gently place it in her bag. Katie looks up at me and smiles. Seeing her on her knees like this makes my cock twitch. I glance away from her and study the room she booked for the night and think how it'd only be a waste to leave the bed unused. "I have about an hour before I have to be somewhere."

"There's a place a few blocks over that has amazing pasta," I tell her.

Katie watches me, and I realize how bad of an idea this really is. It'd be so easy to slip into her panties and show her a good time, but if Jacob found out, he'd murder me. As I'm fantasizing about rustling in the sheets with her, my phone goes off, pulling me away. I glance down and see it's Rachel, and one thing I've learned over the years is to answer her damn call—always. Otherwise, she's a terror to deal with because the woman has the patience of an angry tiger.

"Shit," I whisper and look up at Katie. "Sorry, I gotta take this."

She glances at her watch. "Maybe we can reschedule this for another time then?"

I give her a smile and a nod and answer the phone as she finishes packing her things.

"Maverick. It's Rachel."

I'm well aware, I want to say but don't.

She continues. "So you know the last book in my series releases in less than three months, and I have Olivia scheduling an extended city tour around the Dallas signing."

I wish she'd get to the point. I already confirmed with her assistant I'd be attending. "Yes, I've already cleared my schedule."

"Well, I wanted to call and reiterate a few things first to make sure we're on the same page." Though Rachel is less than friendly most of the time, the seriousness in her tone is almost frightening.

I chuckle, waiting for her to continue because the silence is deafening.

"I'm sure I don't have to explain to you how important it is not to fraternize with my readers or my assistant, Olivia."

Katie stands around, waiting for me to finish my conversation, but this is going to take longer than even I expected. Rachel keeps talking, and eventually, Katie waves goodbye, leaving me alone in the room.

Rachel Meadows has officially cockblocked me.

As she goes into detail about her expectations, I interrupt her.

"Rachel. Hold on. You don't have to keep going. None of that is going to happen. I know the do's and don'ts when it comes to traveling and being on the job. I'm sure you mean well, and I know how other models can be, but I understand the importance of being professional at all times, especially in public settings. I'm not going to arrive late to the events and don't plan on sleeping with anyone. You have nothing to worry about. Trust me."

"Good. That's exactly what I want to hear." She actually sounds relieved. I can only imagine how many different scenarios she's made up about this trip and all the things that could go wrong. I refuse to be an issue, especially considering how high-profile she is. I'm sure Rachel could ruin me.

"I'm still working out your compensation with my publisher, and once everything is confirmed, my assistant will finalize all the fine details with you. Okay?"

"Alright, that sounds great," I tell her.

"I'll see you soon. And Maverick, just remember to be on your best behavior."

I want to explain to her that she doesn't own me regardless of the contract I signed, but she's paid me well, and I'm grateful for the opportunity. So I just agree. We say our goodbyes, and I grab my suit jacket and slip it on. Rachel doesn't take bullshit from anyone, and she won't take it from me. She tends to be straightforward without a filter, and over the past few years, I've learned how to handle her. Pick your battles because you will always lose when going against Rachel.

Not everyone can deal with her no-bullshit attitude, but I'm used to it. She was very particular about which photos were used on her covers, and even though she has a major publisher, what she suggests pretty much goes. The perks of being a best seller, I suppose. Every photo shoot I've had, she's been there to give direction to the photographer. It's annoying, but I get it. She takes her job seriously and wants to be involved in every step.

I look around the empty hotel room, tuck my phone in my pocket, and head out the door, walking down the hallway toward the elevator. Katie's long gone by now, and I'm not one to look desperate. Truthfully, it's probably best we didn't have dinner — especially with the way she was looking at me. Over the years, I've learned how to read a woman like a book. Not to mention, her big brother would have kicked my ass from here to New York if I brought her back to my apartment because things would've inevitably escalated. Pasta, wine, and the next thing she'd be in my bed as I give her the time of her life. Not a good idea.

As soon as I step into the elevator, a long-legged brunette eyes me from head to toe. Women love a man in a fitted suit, and I use it to my advantage each time I wear it, though I really don't need to. Her skirt barely covers her ass, and the heels she's wearing put her at eye level with me. I flash her a sultry smirk before the doors close. Lust swirls around in the elevator, and I watch her breasts rise and fall as I stand next to her. Her breath hitches when I shove my hands into my front pockets.

"Big plans tonight?" I ask her, trying to be polite, though my thoughts are anything but.

Her pouty red lips slightly part then close as if she's trying to find her words.

"Just grabbing a few drinks." She looks over at me, in a cute, sexy way. "I'm Haley."

"Maverick." I smile, reaching a hand out to her. "Nice to meet you, Haley."

Her chocolate brown eyes meet mine, and as she shakes my hand, electricity flows between us. I don't believe in love at first sight, but lust? I definitely believe in lust at first sight.

"I know this sounds forward, but…" I watch as she bites her lower lip. "Would you like to join me?" she asks, bravely.

I chuckle, glancing down at her hand before releasing it to check for a wedding ring. I may enjoy having fun and meeting people, but I draw the line at unavailable women.

"Actually, I was supposed to have dinner with a friend, but my plans got canceled. So, why the hell not?" I give her another signature grin, so she knows I'm down to have a good time with whatever she has in mind.

The elevator reaches the lobby, and the doors slide open. Haley walks out and looks over her shoulder, catching me as I take a glimpse of her perfectly round ass. I swear she's purposely shaking her hips as I walk behind her. She walks to the hotel bar, her heels clicking on the marble floor. It's late afternoon, and the lights are already turned down low to set the mood. A beautiful woman mixed with alcohol is a dangerous concoction, but I go with the flow and pull out the stool next to her and sit.

"Old Fashioned, please," she politely tells the bartender.

"Same," I say. "So you like whiskey?" I turn to her.

"If I'm being honest, it's my kryptonite," she admits with a smirk.

I tilt my head at her. "A beautiful woman is mine."

She laughs as the bartender sets our drinks down. Immediately, she takes a sip. When she sets down the glass, she hooks her finger in and pulls the cherry out, then pops it between her ruby red lips before crushing it with her teeth.

Fuck. She's pulling out all the stops. Tease.

As I reposition my body, my knee brushes against hers. I

place my hand on her thigh, and she scoots closer. The smell of her perfume is intoxicating as it surrounds me.

"So tell me about you, Haley." I take a swig of whiskey, allowing it to burn as it works its way down.

"I'm here for a business conference. Fly out tomorrow afternoon," she says. "I'm not married or anything either; in case you were wondering."

I burst out into laughter. "I wasn't." I'd already confirmed that much by no ring on her finger, but I've been involved with women who've purposely slipped their wedding ring off. I said I try not to sleep with married women; I didn't say I haven't—unintentionally, of course.

"What about you?" she asks, taking another drink of her Old Fashioned.

"I live here. Not married either, in case *you* were wondering. Absolutely one hundred percent single. I'm too focused on my career to get into a serious relationship. I like to have fun. Surf. Workout."

She smiles. "I can appreciate that." Haley narrows her eyes at me. "So, are you like some sort of player or something?"

Now I really laugh. "Truthfully, maybe a tad." I have no reason to lie to her, not when she's flying out tomorrow. Sometimes one-night stands like this are the easiest because there's no expectation of the next day, or ever.

She taps her glass against mine and smiles. "Same."

I kinda figured she was, just by how open she was in the elevator, asking me to join her, and being dressed like that. I've met women like her before; they're a certain breed, and they usually put my playboy tactics to shame. She's beautiful and could have any man she wants, but tonight she chose me. It's painfully obvious where the night is heading.

I finish my drink and order another one. Haley does the same. We make small talk, keeping what we share with each other general. Three whiskeys in, or maybe it's four, and I'm feeling the alcohol stream through my system. Probably should've eaten before we started hammering drinks down, but that would've been the responsible thing to do.

After an hour, Haley leans over and wraps my tie around her fist, pulling me closer to her. "I'd like to take this off you," she whispers in my ear.

Gently, I move the hair from her shoulders. "I'm pretty sure I can help make that happen."

My lips brush against the shell of her ear, which causes her to shiver. Haley removes her tight hold on my tie but continues to lean into me.

"You two want more drinks?" the bartender asks. By the look on his face, he knows where this is leading to as well. I glance at Haley, and she shakes her head and licks her lips.

I hand over my credit card and take care of the tab before standing.

"My room?" she asks with a seductive smile playing on her lips.

I nod, placing my hand on the small of her back, allowing her to lead the way. By the time we make it to the elevator, we're unable to keep our hands off each other.

"I knew from the moment I saw you, I wanted to fuck you," she admits, the whiskey making her lips loose. I grab her ass in my hands and crash my lips against hers as the elevator doors close, and we're shot to the top level. Sometimes it's not easy looking this good, but it definitely has its advantages. Tonight Haley happens to be one of them.

CHAPTER THREE

OLIVIA

THREE MONTHS LATER

"OLIVIA, REPEAT IT TO ME AGAIN," Rachel insists. "From start to finish."

I force a smile and grab the "Bible" in front of me. Though I have her itinerary memorized and we've gone through this several times already, I flip open the planner and read it aloud.

"Friday night before the Dallas signing, you'll do a private meet and greet with members from your reader group. It's from six to eight, and appetizers will be served. Drinks will also be available at the bar. We have fifty give-away bags that include a canvas tote with a book quote printed on the outside, a T-shirt in their size with your author logo, and other pieces of swag items from the Bayshore Coast series."

"And Maverick?" she asks without a beat.

"He'll be there to sign anything they have for him as well

as take pictures with the readers. That's what most of them voted on aside from the striptease I vetoed."

The corner of Rachel's lips tilts just slightly. "They're a feisty bunch."

I hold back a snort. That's an understatement. They're certainly fun, though — I've been an admin in her social media Facebook group for a while now and schedule posts in there from time to time when Rachel is deep in edits.

"The signing starts at eleven on Saturday morning, so I'll come down an hour beforehand with Maverick to set up your table while you're getting your hair and makeup done. You'll need to be down by 10:45 for the author photo. The VIP ticket holders and volunteers are allowed early entrance at 11:00 to get their books signed and photographs taken before the event starts at noon. There isn't a lunch break, so I have room service scheduled to deliver brunch at ten."

"Don't forget about my dietary restrictions."

"I didn't. Low carb, gluten free. I double-checked with the concierge this morning to make sure it's prepared correctly."

To say Rachel Meadows is high maintenance is like saying water is wet. Obvious.

"I also packed snacks for the signing in case you get hungry."

"Great. I'll chow down on a protein bar in front of a line of readers." She inhales a sharp, unsatisfied breath.

"You can take a five-minute bathroom break and eat it then, if needed," I tell her, so she doesn't get anxious about it. "The signing goes until five. You'll get an hour to relax, and then you have a six o'clock dinner meeting with Queen B's Blog."

I continue with the rest of the ten-day schedule that

consists of meet and greets, VIP parties, signings, and meetings between three cities. I worked my ass off to make sure she'd stay busy and get the most out of this trip.

Maybe a little of it was because the busier she is, the busier Maverick will be, and the less I'll have to "watch" him between events. It's already bad enough she's made him my responsibility. However, according to my photographer friend, Presley, who shoots at bookish events, the fans need to be watched just as much. She's told me some stories about women going wild over models and basically giving them lap dances.

I shudder at the image. Mostly because I can't imagine acting like that with a guy I just met. Sure, he has the classic, panty-melting look—chiseled jawline, six-pack (or hell, maybe even an eight-pack), dreamy eyes, and a come-hither smolder, but that doesn't mean I'd even remotely consider throwing myself at him.

God. The more I think about all this, the more I want to start dry heaving and tell her I'm too sick to go. I suck in a deep breath and pretend to sniffle. Is that a cold I feel coming on?

I haven't been sick in three years. It'd be *way* too convenient to get something now. Maybe if I hang out in the emergency room for a weekend, I could catch a nice infection that would get me out of this trip. Summer flu is a real thing.

Would that be going too far?

Absolutely.

Shit, shit, shit.

Rushing around my apartment while yanking my shirt over my head, I trip over something and have to hop on one foot until I find my bearings.

Fuck me, that hurt.

I look at the shoe that nearly assaulted me, and instead of chucking it out the window into traffic like I want, I decide there's no time for that and grab my bags. I've been packed for this trip for the past week but had to add some of my toiletries this morning and nearly had to jump on my suitcase to get it to zip up all the way. Today I'm flying to Los Angeles to meet Maverick Kingston, and I'm already dreading it. *Fuck my life.*

As soon as I'm on the sidewalk, I reach for my phone and realize it's not in my back pocket.

Oh, come on. *Not today!*

I am never, *never* late, and I'm not about to start now. I might not be graceful getting from point A to point B, but I refuse to get off schedule. My Uber is already on the way to take me to the airport so I arrive at my gate on time.

Dragging my bags with me, I rush back up to my apartment, scramble to unlock my door, and look around for my cell.

"Ring, dammit! Ring!" My phone constantly goes off

with texts and emails from Rachel, yet it's conveniently dead silent now.

I search the table, kitchen counter, and dig between the couch cushions, then rush to my bedroom and search the bed, chair, floor. Nothing. *Fuck.*

"Okay, I can figure this out…" I stop and remind myself because if I don't focus, I'm never going to find it and I'll end up missing my ride. "I just need to retrace my steps." I walk back down the hall, glare at the shoe I tripped over, look around the area where my bags were before leaving, and then go to the kitchen.

Wait…

I made coffee this morning before my shower. Opening the fridge door, I sigh in relief when I see my phone next to the bottle of creamer. Quickly grabbing it, I shut the door and grab my suitcases. By some miracle, I make it to the street just as my Uber pulls up.

Thank God.

The gentleman puts everything in the trunk. I'm thankful for his help because one of my suitcases weighs nearly fifty pounds. Preparing to be away from home for two weeks wasn't easy. I won't have much time to do laundry since I'll be catering to Rachel's every need, so I had to pack for every occasion and include a variety of shoes. This isn't a pleasure trip, which means I'll be expected to wear business attire until I'm finished for the day and can hide away in my room for the night.

Not only did I have to get my own things together, but I also spent the past three days packing Rachel's bags and triple-checking our itinerary and reservations. It took five twelve-hour days to nail down her tour events and dates. Considering she only gave me three months' notice meant I had to kiss ass and beg for locations to squeeze us in. On top of that, I had to find hotels that allowed animals since she plans to travel with Angel. Of course, when she's in meetings or too busy, she expects me to feed the little devil and take her outside.

Have I mentioned how I'm not looking forward to being the babysitter bitch during this trip?

Even though I had to plead for space and accommodations for each event and worked day and night to get it all situated, Rachel insisted on re-confirmations even after I assured her everything would go off without a hitch several times.

Once I repeated everything to her yesterday afternoon, I left early to get my things in order. I'd asked my neighbor across the hall to keep an eye on my place and let her know I'd be gone for a couple of weeks. As a retired school teacher in her sixties, Margie's always trying to hook me up with old guys from her book club. She nearly had a heart attack when I explained I'd be gone for that long and had to explain it was a work trip. Just another reminder I should probably get out more.

I make it to O'Hare International Airport and arrive at my gate with plenty of time to spare. I made sure to arrive early just in case security was backed up. Even after stopping for coffee and a pastry, I had an hour to work on my laptop before I boarded.

The flight was four hours long, and considering I stayed up late to finish packing and cleaning my apartment, I slept for the final two hours of the trip. I was able to read for a bit, but I was too anxious about having to meet Maverick Kingston in person to really focus on the words.

Playboy. Arrogant. Cocky and full of himself.

Those are just a few of the traits I'd heard from Presley. She's well known in the book community for her photography skills and for having a huge following on Instagram. She takes extravagant bookish pictures and travels a ton. Presley knows everything there is to know about the drama between authors, readers, bloggers, and models. Anytime I need insider info, I just text her, and she has the full details within twenty minutes.

As soon as I land in LA, I text Maverick to let him know I'm here and that we need to meet up before we start our road trip to Dallas tomorrow.

Olivia: I just arrived at LAX. Can you meet at 4?

That gives me just enough time to check in to my hotel and freshen up.

Maverick: Sure, babe. Wear black leather pants and a red G-string. Don't forget the whip.

What in the ever-loving fuck? I narrow my eyes as I read his message and am certain he meant that for someone else.

25

Olivia: I sincerely hope you're joking. This is Olivia Carpenter, Rachel's assistant. I'm here to pick you up for her tour...

Maverick: So...you want me to bring the whip instead?

I groan internally.
This is going to be a fucking nightmare.

CHAPTER FOUR

MAVERICK

I'M NOT PARTICULARLY LOOKING FORWARD to meeting Miss Uptight Goody-Two-shoes, but she insists on meeting face-to-face before we leave tomorrow, as if I need to know how serious she is about this damn schedule. I offered to pick her up from the airport this morning, but she refused, stating she had rented a car and was more than capable of taking care of herself. Truthfully, Olivia is already rubbing my balls raw, and I've only spoken with her on the phone and through email. She's warned and threatened me in a passive-aggressive way several times about being on my best behavior. I roll my eyes just thinking about the conversations we've had since I confirmed I'd be attending Rachel's extended tour. Olivia's been professional and to the point, but recently, the amount of detail in her emails have made my head spin. The woman has reiterated the schedule so many times, I feel like I could recite it by heart, word for word.

After I get ready for the day and run some errands, I spend my afternoon working out, because staying in the best shape possible is necessary for my profession. I eat healthy, lift weights five times a week, and even run on most days too. One of my only requirements for this trip was for whatever hotel we stayed in to have a gym with weights because I planned to continue my workouts while on the road. Luckily, Rachel backed me on that one so Olivia couldn't argue it.

After I finish at the gym, I head home to take a shower and get ready to meet Olivia. She was dead set on going to a *public* place—a coffee shop not too far from the airport—and refused the invitation to come to my apartment. It's official, she's a prude, which I knew after the first time I spoke with her.

Once I'm out of the shower, I slip on a pair of jeans and a T-shirt and then step outside and schedule an Uber so I can catch up on some emails. Word has gotten out in the book world that my exclusivity expires after this summer, so photographers are desperately trying to book me. For the past few weeks, I've had an autoresponder send a message saying I will return all emails when I get back from traveling. Right now it's too overwhelming to deal with. Maybe I need an Olivia in my life too? If she can handle Rachel Meadows' intense schedule and attitude, the woman can pretty much handle anyone.

As the Uber pulls up, I hop inside and get lost in my phone. LA is a bitch to get through most of the time, so instead of struggling through bumper-to-bumper traffic, I prefer being in the back of a car so I can take care of business.

I read over the last email Olivia sent so it's fresh in my mind. She made it a point to stress we needed to meet at four on the dot, so I purposely arrive late just to test the waters from the get-go, regardless of first impressions and all that. Give me an inch, and I'll take a mile every single day.

When I walk into the coffee shop, I look around for an older, gray-haired woman and am pleasantly surprised when the only person in sight is a cute, uptight, sassy blonde with a scowl permanently fixated on her face.

Olivia Carpenter isn't eighty, which is shocking considering the way she acts.

I smile. She rolls her eyes.

And just like that, we're off to a good start.

Instead of rushing immediately toward her, I walk to the counter and take my time ordering a black coffee. Once the cup is handed over to me, I sit in front of her with a smirk. "Olivia?"

She looks down at her watch, then back at me unamused. "I said four. Not four twenty-five."

I chuckle. Studying her. Already noticing her quirks. She's the Hermione Granger of author assistants with her planners stacked high in front of her, clothes perfectly pressed, and every button done up to her neck. Not a wisp of sandy blond hair is out of place from the bun tightly fixated on the back of her head, and she sits up straight as a board. I swear if the wind blows the wrong way, she'll tip over.

I glance down at the bottle of water she's drinking. "Who comes to a coffee house and drinks water?"

"I've had my daily allowance of caffeine already, thank you very much. Now, can we get down to business? I'm not one for small talk." *No kidding.*

I'm actually taken aback by the way she's treating me within the first thirty seconds of meeting me. Not many women blow me off like this, which makes me wonder if my charm is fading. It's true, some women are immune to it, and Olivia already seems like she's going to be a tough egg to crack. Then again, I'm always up for a good challenge.

I rub my hand across the scruff on my chin. "Sure thing. I'm ready to listen to you go over this *again*. But let me say this; when I close my eyes, all I can see is your three-page email detailing every second of my life for the next twelve days. But please, Miss Priss, continue."

She ignores my frustration and opens a notebook where she has everything written out in the neatest handwriting I've ever seen with bullet points, timelines, and dates. My phone vibrates as she starts reading off our insane schedule, and I check a text message and respond. Instantly, she stops and stares at me. It's actually the most attention she's given me since I sat down.

"Are you even listening to me?" Her green eyes bore into me.

"Are you hungry? Do you need a Snickers? You seem a little cranky." I tuck my phone in my pocket and give her a shit-eating grin.

She slams her notebook shut and glares at me. "This was obviously a huge mistake. I really hope I don't kill you before the end of this. I value my job, and a murder rap wouldn't look good for me."

I chuckle, which only seems to set her off even more. "I'm sure Rachel and her raving fans wouldn't appreciate that. I'm willing to bet they'd go on a witch hunt if that happened."

Olivia huffs and interlocks her fingers together on the table. She looks like she wants to stand and strangle me but somehow shows great restraint. "Rachel expects you to be on your very best behavior during this tour because you're representing her brand, which she's worked very hard to establish over the last decade. That means you are required to arrive on time to all events. You need to be presentable and friendly to her readers. And you have to keep your dick in your pants. I know all this is going to be really hard for you, but those are the rules, and my job is to make sure you follow them. Understand? I've been voluntold to be your babysitter or truant officer—maybe both. So don't test me and everything will be just fine."

"Babysitter? That's hilarious!" I laugh and take a sip of coffee. "I don't need watching, though. I'm a big boy," I respond sarcastically.

"I've heard how some models act at these events. I've been made well aware of your kind, Mr. Playboy," she adds.

My eyebrows pop up. "Oh really? Please enlighten me then, Miss Priss. I'd love to know what preconceived notions you have about me so I can make them *allllllll* come true in the next twelve days," I taunt, taking another swig of coffee.

"*Stop* calling me that," Olivia demands between gritted teeth. We've been around each other for approximately ten minutes, and I've already managed to permanently smash in her buttons. *Perfect.* This is going to be fun.

"Are you always this arrogant?" she asks.

"Are you always so uptight?" I fire right back.

She shakes her head. "This is an absolute nightmare. We're done here."

Olivia stands up and grabs her notebooks and planners. She presses them against her chest and glares at me.

Instantly, I stand too. "Great talk."

She groans and walks toward the door, and I follow, checking her out in the process. Olivia is tall, though she's wearing heels. Her black skirt hugs her tiny waist and accentuates her curves. She looks like she just walked out of an episode of *Law & Order* with how put together she is. I chuckle at her expense and continue to follow her to the car that's perfectly parallel parked. As she unlocks it and sets her library of planners in the passenger seat, I stop.

"Please tell me you didn't rent a fucking Toyota Prius for a long road trip."

She turns on her heels and takes a step toward me. "Or what?"

"It's seriously one of the shittiest cars a person can rent for someone my size. You couldn't have gotten something more comfortable or spacious? I'm six foot two, for crying out loud."

"And when you're cramping, think about the amazing gas mileage we're going to get and the money we're going to save by going hybrid." For the first time all day, she smiles, but it's smug as fuck. Almost as if she gets some sick satisfaction out of the fact I will be tortured for the next two weeks. I'm pretty sure she does.

I swallow hard. I'm actually pissed. "Well then, I might have to call Rachel and let her know I won't be able to make it after all."

Olivia narrows her eyes at me, and I see a glimpse of panic flash across her face. "You wouldn't."

Tilting my head, I cross my arms across my chest. "Test me." I repeat her words from earlier, throwing them back in her face just to see if she'll combust with anger.

"If you did that…" She stops herself and bites her tongue, so she doesn't continue.

"What? What are you going to do?"

We stand there and stare at each other before Olivia relents. "Fine, whatever. Didn't realize we were using threats here. You have *no idea* what you just started, Maverick."

"Whatever it is, I promise you, I'll finish it, *Miss Priss*."

She shakes her head and climbs into the shitty Prius

mumbling something under her breath, and I'm pretty sure I heard her call me an asshole. Before starts the car, she rolls down the passenger window but refuses to look at me.

"I'll be at your house at seven. Don't make me wait." As I watch her drive away and turn in the absolute wrong direction, I let out a laugh. I may have pushed Olivia's buttons, but she's managed to push mine right back. The next two weeks of my life are going to be a lot more interesting than I originally thought, and I'm sure she's thinking the same.

I look up at the cloudless blue sky, and a smile fills my face. Someone better say a prayer for Olivia because now I'm even more determined to wear her down to the bone, and I have a week and a half to do it.

Challenge accepted.

CHAPTER FIVE

OLIVIA

MAVERICK KINGSTON MANAGED to get under my skin in less than an hour and then showed up in my dreams last night.

Not by choice.

Ugh! The man is infuriating. He doesn't take anything seriously and treats life like one big frat party. So, the next eleven days should be a blast.

After his not-so-subtle threat about not going on this road trip in a Prius, I had no choice but to replace the rental car. Driving with him will be painful enough. I don't need to hear him complain the whole time about the damn car.

Once I grab some coffee, I head over to Maverick's place and text him.

Olivia: I'm here. Use the bathroom before you come out. Our first stop isn't for five hours.

Maverick: Don't worry, babe. I'll bring a bottle of water and reuse it ;)

I groan, almost wishing I'd kept the Prius now.

Sipping on my coffee, I adjust the radio and play something mellow. It helps me relax, and if I'm going to be driving in LA traffic this early, I'll need to stay calm.

"Well, well, well…" I hear Maverick say in a singsong voice. He throws his luggage into the back and flashes me a victorious smile as he climbs into the passenger side. "Nice wheels."

"You didn't leave me much choice," I grind out. "Also, do you have something against being on time?"

"This is California, babe. We're a chill type of people here."

"Stop calling me babe," I tell him harshly as I pull onto the road. The GPS is already set, and it says we're twelve hours from our first hotel. This is going to be a long, miserable day. "I'm not *your* babe, and my name is Olivia."

"Well, *Olivia.* You aren't in Kansas anymore. You can lose the bitter, uptight attitude."

I scrunch my nose. I don't even know what that's supposed to mean. "I'm from Chicago."

He snorts, adjusting his seat and shifting it back to make room for his long legs. "That definitely explains it."

I roll my eyes though I'm not looking at him.

"Can I turn off this church music?" Maverick asks thirty minutes into our trip. He leans forward and starts messing with the knob.

"It's nice driving music," I argue, swatting his hand away.

"You can't be serious. This shit is gonna put you to sleep, and then we're going to crash and die. You really want that on your conscience?"

The corner of his lips tilts up just the slightest.

"Guess it wouldn't matter. I'd be dead." I flash a smug smile right back at him.

"Oh, I see how it is. You look all innocent and smart, but deep down, you have this morbidity to you."

I shoot him a look. "You're the morbid one with all your crashing and dying talk." I turn my music back on. "Now no more talking about it because if I don't get you to these events on time, Rachel *will* actually kill me."

"Why you so scared of her anyway? I could fit her in my pocket. She looks harmless enough."

Glancing at him, I shake my head, then force myself to focus on the road. "You know she's anything but harmless."

He chuckles, shaking his head. "Yeah, you're right. She's not a firecracker like you, though."

"I'm not even sure what that means, but you can't label me when you've just met me."

"Oh, like you haven't labeled me already?"

"I know your kind. I've heard plenty about you to form an opinion," I tell him with purpose.

"God, you're so hypocritical. You think you're the first prissy, stick-up-her-ass assistant I've met? Doesn't mean I know *you* just like it doesn't mean you know *me*."

He kinda has a point, but I don't tell him that. His ego is already taking up all the space in the car.

Ignoring his comment, I grip the steering wheel a bit tighter. We're in heavy traffic, and I'm not used to eight-lane highways.

"You better change lanes," he says.

"I'm trying." I look over my shoulder, searching for a spot to move into.

"Might wanna try the blinker. I heard it's a signal for other drivers to know you want to turn or move over."

36

I sigh and put it on. He's distracting me.

"Stay quiet so I can focus."

His chuckles are the last thing I hear from him as I attempt to move across the lanes. Finally, I make it, and we coast down the highway in silence until the city is behind us.

"When are we stopping for food?" He speaks up for the first time in hours. I look over at him and see he's sticking out his lower lip, making a pouty face. "I'm shriveling to nothing over here." He slightly lifts his shirt and pats his ridiculously cut stomach.

His eyes meet mine, and I quickly look away although he saw me staring. Swallowing, I look at the GPS to see how much farther until our first stop.

"We have about an hour left," I tell him. "Think you'll manage to stay alive for that long?"

He groans loudly, and it makes me laugh. I quickly catch myself and stop.

"You have a nice laugh. It's a pleasant change from your short fuse and snarl."

"I don't snarl!" I argue. "I just like having a plan and sticking to it."

He noticeably rolls his eyes. "Okay, Miss Priss. Letting your hair down won't kill ya."

"No, but your arrogant, self-absorbed attitude just might," I throw at him, holding back a smirk.

"Well, I think that's debatable. Most of the women I date think it's charming."

A loud snort bursts out of me, and I'm unable to bite my tongue. "I think that says more about *who* you're dating than anything. They must be desperate."

"Damn, what a burn." He chuckles. "Adding hostile to your personality resume."

I inhale a deep breath, realizing that was a really mean thing to say. "Okay, sorry. That wasn't nice. But I'm not taking back what I said about you. You're arrogant, and there's no denying that."

"Oh, well then, thanks, I guess." He smirks. "You say it like being arrogant is a bad thing, though. In my profession, I kinda have to be. I'm constantly selling myself to photographers and showing them I'm worthy of being in their magazines and advertisements. If I don't act confident and prove I'm the best guy for the gig, I'll lose it to the thousands of other people pursuing the job."

I think about his words for a minute. "Okay, well I can certainly understand that. But I think you're just naturally that way." I shrug, biting down on my lower lip so he doesn't see right through me. He has every right to be confident; there's no doubt about that. He's got it all—the body, the face, the perfect white teeth and smile. His abs are plastered all over Rachel's covers and book promo graphics. He even has that annoying muscular V that trails from his hips to down below his waistline. *Annoyingly sexy.* "However, that doesn't mean you can't be humble in other aspects of your life."

"That's a pretty big accusation for someone you just met. How do you know I'm not? You haven't been around me long enough to know anything about me. Don't you think?"

Damn. He's right. "Fine. Prove me wrong then."

An hour later, we're stopped at a little family diner for lunch, and I'm ready to suck down another gallon of coffee. At this point, I'm not even sure caffeine affects me, but I'm an addict, so I enjoy the taste too.

The hostess smiles wide at Maverick as soon as he walks in, and her demeanor changes when she sees me following behind him. She studies me hard, eyes lingering up and down my body as if she's disgusted a guy like him would be with a girl like me.

As we follow her to a table, I look down at my outfit and wonder what the judgmental snob was thinking about me. This is one of my favorite pantsuits, so she obviously has zero taste.

"Here you go." She places the menus down in front of us once we sit across from each other in the booth. "The lunch special is the turkey and avocado wrap, and the soup is French onion."

"Sounds great, thank you," Maverick says, giving her a million-dollar smile. I fight back the urge to groan loudly. She acts like I'm not sitting here and talks directly to him while smiling and giggling like a fool. No one is that excited about lunch specials.

"Your server will be right with you."

Maverick flashes her a quick wink before she trails off. I stare at him, dumbfounded.

"What?" He smirks.

I roll my eyes and grab a menu.

"What was that for?"

"Don't you think that was a tad inappropriate?" I ask, not looking up at him as I scan the menu.

"Inappropriate? How? You're gonna tell me how to act before we even get to the event?" His voice is gruff and laced with annoyance.

"Because I'm sitting right here, across from you, and she acted like I didn't exist. We could've been on a date for all she knows."

His brows shoot up, eyes widening.

"That didn't come out right. That's not what I meant. No, I mean like —"

"Olivia, stop." He chuckles. "You're cute when you're all flustered."

I narrow my eyes at his statement. "Don't call me cute. And I'm not flustered."

"And that's exactly how she knew we weren't on a date. Could probably smell the distaste you have for me the second you walked in." He smirks to tell me he thinks he's funny.

"Alright, but still. It's rude to ignore a customer and hit on the other one. So unprofessional," I assert.

Maverick shakes his head while smiling and lifts his menu. "She's a hostess with a low-cut top and six-inch platforms. I doubt she was aiming for professionalism at all."

Our waitress finally comes over, and we order. I'm so hungry, I ask for crackers while we wait for our food.

"You gonna eat that?" Maverick nods to the other half of my club sandwich twenty minutes later.

"No, I can't. I'm stuffed." I had soup before my meal because I was starving, but now I just want a nap.

"Sweet. Can I have it?"

My eyes widen, shocked he's still hungry after shoveling an entire steak into his mouth. "Are you serious?"

Maverick reaches over and grabs it from my plate. "Gotta feed those muscles." He shoots me a wink — to annoy me, I'm sure. He should know by now it has zero effect on me, yet he enjoys testing me.

"Sure," I say, laughing when he doesn't wait for my answer before taking a large bite. "I can't believe how much you eat considering how fit you are."

He reaches for his water and takes a long swig before setting it back down. "So you think I'm fit, huh?"

Rolling my eyes, I take my napkin and throw it at his smug expression. "That's like saying the sky is blue, so don't get any ideas in that big head of yours."

After paying, Maverick yanks the keys from my hand and says it's his turn to drive. I don't bother arguing with him this time.

"I'm going to use the bathroom again before we go," I tell him, so he doesn't wait for me. "You might want to as well."

"I went when we got here. So did you."

"I know, but it's better to be safe than sorry. We aren't stopping again for a few hours," I remind him.

"I'm fine. Meet you at the car."

Shaking my head, I drop the subject and go about my business. I told him earlier we were only making one more stop after lunch to fill up so we'll arrive at the hotel around eight tonight. Though I didn't want to be in the car for twelve hours today, it was necessary. As long as we stay on schedule, making it to Dallas on time tomorrow shouldn't be an issue.

"So since I'm driving, my radio now," Maverick says the moment I sit in the passenger seat.

"Is this where you tell me you're secretly into Ariana Grande and Avril Lavigne?"

"First off, no. Secondly, Avril is a killer punk singer, so joke's on you." He grins, fiddling with the stations.

"Yeah, clearly." I groan, buckling in and trying to mentally prepare myself for the next six hours with this man.

"AC/DC, baby!"

I furrow my brows and scowl, wishing I'd brought headphones with me.

An hour goes by, and instead of dwelling on his horrible music choices, I write in my notebooks and planner, making a list of the things I need to do in order of importance before this trip is over. Rachel has continued to pile on tasks, and if I can complete some of them during the next week and a half, that'll save me from being overloaded when we return.

Just as I'm writing down some notes about her next release, I see Maverick nearly dancing in his seat and looking over his shoulder to merge to the right lane.

"What are you doing?" I look around and see we haven't traveled very far since lunch.

"I need to piss. I saw a sign for an outlet mall coming up."

I look at the time. We don't need gas for a couple more hours.

"I told you to go at the diner!" I scold. "We don't have time to stop. We're already behind schedule since Miss Hostess with no shame chatted with you for an extra five minutes."

He turns his head and glares at me. "So you're going to punish me by making me piss myself?"

"Surely you can hold it for a couple of hours."

"Olivia."

"Maverick."

"I'm driving, and I'm taking this exit."

"No!" I hold my hand to stop him from turning the steering wheel. "Those stores are probably packed. By the time we find a parking spot, you find a bathroom, and we drive out of the traffic, it'll waste twenty minutes!"

"Take your hand off the wheel, Olivia. You'll make us get into an accident."

"Fine," I grit between my teeth. "Keep driving then."

"I will as soon as I take a leak."

"Argh! Why are you so difficult? I just want to get to the

hotel and take a hot shower and sleep before we have to do this all over again tomorrow."

"And you will, so stop being so dramatic."

"Maverick, seriously." I hold up my planner to show him the schedule. "We'll run right into the evening rush hour, and that'll fuck it all up."

He narrows his eyes as if he's actually reading it, and I'm so distracted by how close he is to me that I don't even see him moving to take it right out of my hand. He presses a button on his door, and the window automatically rolls down.

"What are you—"

"You wanna know how I feel about your fucking schedule?"

My eyes widen in fear. "You wouldn't."

"Wanna find out?" He quirks a brow, taunting me as he shifts it closer to the window. Watching the pages flutter in the breeze causes my heart to race. This can't be happening; my entire life is in there, and so is Rachel's.

"Give it back! That's my 'bible!'"

He laughs. Fucking laughs!

I know I'm not the easiest person to be around. It's probably why I don't have many friends or a social life, but this is just plain mean.

"I will junk punch you with no mercy if you don't hand it over, Maverick." I hold down my stare as I put one hand out for him to place it there.

"Damn, Miss Priss. Taking it to that level, huh?" He flashes a smirk, obviously not too worried about my threat.

My jaw drops open. "You started it!"

He shakes his head and chuckles as he tosses it on my lap, ignoring my hand.

Moments later, he takes the exit and finds a parking spot —which takes forever just as I suspected.

"Be back in a second," he says as he opens the door and steps out. When I don't respond, he leans into the car, and continues, "Let me know if you need help getting that stick out of your ass later. I'm assuming it's wedged pretty deep, so I'll buy some lube just in case."

Vibration at the back of my throat releases a deep growl. Gah! He's so infuriating.

I look up and see a wide, proud smile plastered on his chiseled face.

"Fuck off."

He chuckles loudly as if he accomplished what he was aiming for—riling me up.

"My offer to junk punch you stands," I remind him. "Hurry up."

"Ooh, I like it when you talk dirty to me." He winks and shuts the door behind him before I can respond.

Leaning back, I fall against the headrest and groan.

One day down, only eleven more to go.

CHAPTER SIX

MAVERICK

OLIVIA'S KNOCKING on my door before the sun rises, which only annoys the shit out of me because it's literally six on the dot. I understand being on a schedule and all, but she's absolutely relentless. I open the door wearing nothing but my boxer briefs, and she glances down at my morning wood, then back up at me.

"For crying out loud," she says. "It's time to go, and you're not even dressed."

I close the door in her face and hear her groans on the other side. I can just imagine her standing there, fuse lit, ready to explode as I throw on some jeans and a T-shirt. Considering we have all day to drive to Dallas and we're thirteen hours away means we don't have to really rush around just as long as we're there by tonight.

By the way she's acting, I can tell she's already wound up tight.

Last night after my shower, I packed everything, so I'm mostly ready to go, but I want her to sweat for a moment.

After five minutes pass, I hear pounding on the door. I'm halfway surprised she waited out there that long.

I grab my suitcase, pop the handle up, and open the door. Olivia rolls her eyes and shakes her head, which only causes me to laugh. I follow her to the elevator. When we step in, she doesn't say a word to me.

"I need the keys. I'm driving." I hold out my hand, and at first, she hesitates but then places them in my palm. I'll take all the small victories I can get.

Before we leave the hotel lobby, Olivia stops at the front desk and hands over the key cards, then asks for her receipt. Instead of waiting, I walk to the car, pop the trunk, and throw my suitcase inside. Soon, she's walking toward me dressed in proper business attire and high heels, which I didn't notice earlier because I was too busy closing the door in her face.

"You're going to wear that to travel?" I look her up and down before taking her suitcases, pushing the handles down, and placing them in the trunk. I try to take her laptop bag, but she refuses to hand it over. I shrug and repeat my question.

"What's wrong with what I'm wearing?" she asks with her arms folded over her chest.

"It's too uptight for a road trip, don't you think?"

She doesn't say a word before she turns on her heels and climbs into the passenger seat. I take my time walking to the driver's side, climb in, adjust the mirrors, then find a rock and roll station on satellite radio, which will be a complete lifesaver when we're driving in the middle of nowhere Texas.

Olivia bends over and starts pulling notebooks from her bag, and when she flips to the daily itinerary she's laid out, I turn up the music because I don't want to hear about our stupid schedule today. Rock music screams through the car, and it takes all of ten seconds for her to reach over and turn it down.

"I can't concentrate with that crap blaring. I'd like to try to get some work done while you drive." She reaches and changes the station to her classical church shit.

I pull out of the hotel parking lot and put the radio back to my music. "When I'm driving, we listen to what *I* want to listen to and vice versa. Road trip rules 101." The Rolling Stones scream out about getting satisfaction. When she goes to turn it down, I lightly swat her hand. "I'm serious."

Olivia slams her planner shut and stares out the window as I pull into a gas station. We're a few miles from the New Mexico border, and I want to fill up now and get some water without her telling me when I'm allowed to drink. "We don't have time to stop right now. We can make it a little farther," she argues, but I don't listen.

Before I get out, she begrudgingly hands me her business credit card, and I fill up the car. She seems to be picking and choosing her battles today, which is pleasant in a way. I might actually start wearing her down. Who knows, by the time we make it to Dallas, we could be friends. I laugh at the thought. Before I get in the car, I run inside the gas station and grab a few bottles of water for us. When I open the door and hand her one, she gives me a smile, actually grateful.

"Thank you." She twists off the top and nearly drinks half of it.

"Dang, girl. Want me to go in and get you another one?" I grin.

She shakes her head, then goes back to her book, and the small moment we shared disappears. I get in the car and turn the radio just loud enough to drown out the road noise.

Desert with patches of random green grass lines the road. I'm thankful the weather is nice and the sky is blue; it makes for easy driving. Soon we're leaving New Mexico and crossing the Texas border. Seeing all the brown really makes me miss the water in California.

Olivia looks around at the nothingness as we drive through El Paso and Van Horn. "Maverick. How much gas do we have?" she asks, going back to her planner.

I look down and see we're under a quarter of a tank, but closer to empty than not. "Enough," I tell her.

"Seriously. I had our gas stops planned out based on mileage, and you ruined that from the get-go. How much gas do we have?" I can tell she's starting to panic the farther we drive away from civilization.

"There's another town coming up. We'll make it there. Quit worrying. I've been road tripping since I was old enough to drive." I point at the GPS and show her the gas symbol in the next town. "There's a gas station in Toyah. We'll make it there, no problem."

Olivia relaxes, but only slightly. I watch the gas meter move closer to empty as we continue to drive. Glancing back at the GPS, I see the gas station is about a mile away and is located next to the post office on the main road. Almost sitting on the edge of her seat, Olivia glances around at the ghost town we're driving through. Old houses and empty buildings line the road. We inch closer to the gas icon on the screen, and I slow to turn into the parking lot only to see the station is closed with windows boarded. There's a faded *For Sale* sign nailed on the outside.

We're literally fucked, and we both know it.

"Now what are we going to do?" She turns to me, and I try to think of something, but I have nothing. So I do what any person would in this situation, and I continue driving until the small town is behind us. Thankfully, there's a pull-off in the distance, and I swing into the rest area which is more like a parking lot than anything considering there are zero bathrooms. Diesel trucks are pulled over with their engines running, the drivers most likely catching some sleep after a long haul. Metal windmills decorate the grassy area, and they spin fast in the wind, but other than that, nothing else is around us. I park in front of a big rig and pull my phone from my pocket and try to figure out our next step. Olivia grabs her phone too. I watch her turn it off and then turn it back on, annoyed with it.

"Please tell me you have cell service," she finally says, worry coating her voice.

"I do," I say, wanting to tell her I'll make this right, but instead, she gets out of the car, slamming the door behind her. Yep, she's pissed. Really pissed, and this time it's more than warranted. With some quick googling, I see there's a gas station twenty-three miles away, but there's no way we'd make it. It's not within walking distance, and I'll be damned if I try to bum a ride from anyone out here. *Texas Chainsaw Massacre* comes to mind.

I get out of the car and walk toward Olivia.

"Why didn't you just listen to me?" The words spew out of her mouth like venom when I get closer.

"I know this is totally my fault, and I'm sorry." I don't want to argue about this because no excuse I can give will even remotely fix this. We're going to be behind schedule now, and I'm grateful she doesn't throw that in my face even though I deserve it. Sometimes I can be too goddamn hard-headed for my own good.

"Apology accepted." She finally lets out a deep breath

and checks her watch. "We're going to have to call roadside assistance. It's the only thing I can think of."

Olivia turns on her heels and walks back to the car. She leans over and pulls the rental contract from the glove compartment and reads through it. After a moment, she finds what she's looking for and shows it to me. It's the 1-800 number for roadside assistance. "I'm so glad I paid extra for this. Also, I don't have cell service, so…"

"I'll take care of it." I put in the number and am transferred to several different people before I'm sent to the right department.

"So where ya located again?" the woman on the line asks in a thick Southern accent.

"In the middle of nowhere." I laugh as I look around. "We're about two miles outside of Toyah, Texas, at a parking area. We're eastbound on I-10."

I hear clicking on a keyboard for a minute. "Ah, found you. Okay, hold, please. I'm gonna try to call around and see if I can get you some help. You weren't lying, sweetie. You really are in the middle of nowhere." She laughs. "Be right back."

I sit on hold for over five minutes, and I'm half worried that we're going to be stranded out here. Different horrible scenarios fill my mind. If we don't make it to Dallas tonight, Rachel will lose her shit, and neither Olivia nor I want that. We have one thing in common, at least.

"Sir, are you still there?" the woman asks, coming back on the line, pulling me away from my thoughts.

"Yeah, I am." I lean against the car and watch Olivia hold up her cell phone to try to find service. She should really loosen up. She's wound up so damn tight.

"So, I've got someone who can come out, but they're

about ninety minutes away. This company is coming from Van Horn, and they're the closest."

"There's a gas station less than thirty miles away in Pecos. There's no one there who can help?" I'm already dreading telling Olivia how much time we're going to lose.

"No, sir. We've got companies we contract with, and they're the closest. I'm sorry. You'll need to make sure you have the rental agreement nearby when he arrives. If he's not there in an hour and a half, then you'll need to call back so we can check to make sure everything is okay. Do you have any more questions?"

"No. Thanks for your help."

She finishes explaining a few details, and then we say our goodbyes. Olivia walks over and gets in the car. I get inside too.

"So?" she asks.

I swallow hard. "An hour and a half."

She tucks her lips in her mouth and closes her eyes tight, and I have a feeling she's trying to control her emotions. Even just being around her this short amount of time, I've learned that she lives and dies by her schedule, so I actually do feel bad.

"We don't have time for this," she finally says, releasing a slow, agitated breath.

"I know," I say as she repositions the seat. I roll down the windows, allowing some sort of breeze to blow through, though it's hot as hell outside. Thirty minutes pass, and it feels like an eternity. My bladder is ready to burst on top of it all. Not able to hold it anymore, I get out of the car.

Olivia sits up. "Where are you going?"

"I gotta take a piss," I tell her, walking across the grass, trying to find some semi-secluded place where I can find relief. I walk across rocks and over patches of grass and find a few trees. What kind of rest area doesn't have a bathroom? Seriously. After I've pissed, I go back to the car and get inside. Olivia has hand sanitizer waiting for me.

"Are you a germaphobe too?" She squirts way too much in my hands.

"No. I just like being prepared."

That's the understatement of the year.

Another thirty minutes pass, and I see Olivia squirming as I scroll through my emails. "What?" I turn and look at her.

"I have to pee now too," she admits.

"There are a few trees over there. It's pretty secluded."

She squeezes her knees together. "I can't pee outside."

I burst out into laughter. "When you're desperate, you'll pee anywhere."

Five minutes pass, and she looks over at me. "Will you go with me and keep watch? I mean, what if someone walks up on me while I'm trying to squat."

I hold back my laughter. "Sure."

She digs in her bag and pulls out a travel size pack of tissues. I follow her across the gravel, and she's having a hell of a time walking in those heels. Instead of saying anything, I just chuckle.

"Shut up," she says, but I can tell she's smiling by her playful tone. Stopping, she looks around, then turns to face me. "I guess this is as good as it's gonna get."

I turn my back and can hear her struggling. Crossing my arms over my chest, I keep a lookout and laugh because she's dressed in business wear with pantyhose and all.

She groans behind me. "Great, now I'm pee shy!"

Eventually, she goes and lets out a sigh of relief. I hear

her clothes rustling behind me as she tries to make herself presentable again, I'm sure.

"Finished?" I ask.

She comes up next to me and stumbles on her heel, causing me to catch her from falling. Olivia nervously looks up into my eyes.

"Next time, jeans, T-shirt, and Chucks when traveling for thirteen hours. Got it, Miss Priss?" I release my hold on her and smile. She smooths her skirt and runs a hand over her hair, then we head back to the car.

Thirty minutes to go and I'm growing more impatient with each passing second. Though I hate that we're in this situation, I can't say I hate being with her. I feel like the two of us are making headway, and her prissiness is beginning to grow on me.

CHAPTER SEVEN

OLIVIA

I LIVE in Chicago for a reason. Texas is hot as hell, and though it's not super humid, I'm pretty sure the sun is baking my skin, which is the last thing I need right now. As I sweat, I realize how bad of an idea it was to put on pantyhose this morning. I should've just worn something comfortable, but it's important for me to look professional on the outside regardless if I'm a hot mess on the inside. I try to control the things I can, and appearance is one of those things. You always dress for the job you want, not the one you have.

Just as I open my phone to check and see if I miraculously have service, I see an old beat-up Chevy truck pull up slowly next to the car. An older guy with a cowboy hat makes eye contact with me, then drives forward and reverses until the bumper is almost against the car. Instantly, I enter panic mode.

I look over at Maverick who's as calm as can be. "Is that the gas delivery?"

He glances at me, then back at the truck. "I have no idea."

My adrenaline spikes, and I realize this is how every horror movie starts. The truck is an older model, and there's no signage on it saying it's a company vehicle. I'm growing more anxious every minute the guy doesn't get out. Seriously, what is he doing? What's taking him so long? Is he busy sharpening his knife or loading his gun?

Eventually, the door swings open with a pop and a screech, causing me to jump. The man's wearing dirty blue jeans that are tucked into some tall worn cowboy boots. The button-up shirt is rolled to his elbows. Yep, we're going to die. I put my window up and buckle my seat belt just in case we have to hurry and drive away. Considering we're basically on empty, we won't get very far. Maverick glances over at me as the man walks toward us and leans against the car.

"Y'all waiting for some gas?" he asks, his voice rough and full of gruff.

"Yes, sir," Maverick says.

"Alright." He returns to his truck, pulls a gas can from the back, and Maverick gets out of the car to help. I let out a breath of relief, because holy shit, why did he feel the need to block us in like that? The whole situation is awkward as hell. I watch Maverick and the guy put the gas in the car from the side mirror. After Maverick signs a document and tips the man, he walks to his truck and pulls away. I suck in a deep breath, needing more oxygen.

Before Maverick walks around to the driver's side, I get out of the car.

"I'm driving the rest of the way." I hold out my hand, and after a moment of hesitation, he hands me the key. I refuse to run out of gas again on this trip especially after I've planned every single stop. I was too focused on my work to notice how far we'd gone, and by the time I did, it was too late. I'm somewhat pissed with myself for not saying something sooner. It's already late afternoon, and we've lost too much time, which means we'll arrive in Dallas well after dark. Not to mention, I have to be up at the butt crack of dawn to pick Rachel up from the airport.

We get in the car at the same time, and I take off down the road. The gas only filled the car up to a quarter of a tank, so as soon as we're in the next town, I fill up. Though I don't want to, because we don't really have time, we stop in Odessa and grab some food, then continue the rest of the way. Once we're back in the car, Maverick leans his seat back and instantly falls asleep for a few hours. Since he's out, I put on an audiobook and listen to it while I drive. I randomly glance over at him, noticing how peaceful he looks when he's sleeping. His chiseled jaw and pouty plump lips are enough to drive any woman crazy. I understand why women flock to him because he's attractive and has that playboy charm. I've been warned about his type, though. I'm determined to keep my eyes on the road and speed up, trying to cut as much time off our trip as possible. Once we get below a half tank, I stop and fill up again. Maverick is sleeping so hard he doesn't even notice.

Once we're back on the road, he lifts his seat, rubs his hands over his face, and looks around, noticing the sun is set. My audiobook is still playing.

He fucks me so hard, and I beg him not to stop. I want and need more of him, and he gives me exactly what I want. I feel as if I'm crumbling under his touch as he... I turn the radio off and am thankful it's dark so he can't see the blush on my cheeks.

"Damn. That's intense," he says. "What the hell were you listening to?"

I swallow. "Rachel's book that just released." I've

already read the book half a dozen times during her revisions and listened to the audiobook for approval, but regardless of Rachel being a hardass, she tells a damn good story.

"Man. Y'all are dirty." He chuckles.

"And this is why all her readers want to meet you." I grin, though he can't see. "They envision you as the male character since you're on the cover. Another reason you need to be on your best behavior. They're fantasizing about Ian, the hero, when they look at you."

He yawns. "I'll take any advantage that I can."

I roll my eyes. As if he needs one.

"Do you want me to drive?" Maverick asks.

I shake my head. "I'm good. We only have an hour before we're there."

"Really? Wow. Good job." He pulls out his phone and scrolls through Facebook. "So what do you do for fun?"

I keep my eyes on the road. "I work a lot. There's no time for fun."

"Seriously? You don't have any hobbies or anything?" He seems shocked by this.

"I like to nap and read. Does that count?"

He shakes his head. "So you're telling me all you do is work, read, and sleep. That's it? You're such a party animal."

Wow, having someone repeat that aloud makes me sound lame.

"I take my job really seriously. I live and breathe Rachel's life and staying on schedule. There's no time for partying, Mr. Playboy."

Maverick snickers, and I'm pretty sure he's laughing *at* me.

My grip tightens on the steering wheel. "What?"

"Nothing." He turns his head and bursts out into laughter.

"Seriously, what?" I ask.

He shrugs. "It's just unbelievable that you're so married to your job. If you don't live a little now, eventually, you'll wake up and wonder what you accomplished in life. From the moment I met you, I knew you were uptight, but this is crazy. I bet this road trip is the most fun you've had in ages."

"I wouldn't call this fun," I snap back, but I know he's right. It's just when Rachel releases a new book, she needs me more than usual, and considering this is the last book in this series that hit the charts for weeks at a time, there's no time for me to have a personal life. That's a part of the job, and I accepted it a long time ago. I'd try to explain myself to him, but there's no reason. We're only going to be together for the next ten days, and that's it. I'm not trying to be his friend.

"That's fair. But at least this is forcing you to live a little. Who knows, by the end of it, maybe you'll appreciate the adventure yo u experienced, even if you hate every minute of it."

I turn up the radio wanting this conversation to end and realize it's still a sex scene in the book and turn it back off. Rachel can write a chapter's worth of sex, and listening to the actors read it aloud makes it sound so much dirtier. Moans and pants are added in, and I cannot listen to that while he's sitting next to me and staring at me.

Eventually, we pull up to the hotel in Dallas, and I couldn't be happier to be here. I hand the car keys to the valet as they unload my bags and offer to take them up to my room. I allow them, knowing they're working for tips, but Maverick takes his own. Once I check into the hotel, I hand him his key card so we can go our separate ways for the night.

"Want to have a drink with me at the bar?" he asks. I can't deny how sexy he looks standing there with big puppy dog eyes. His tongue swipes his pouty lips, and I force myself to look away. If I weren't on the clock and he wasn't Maverick Kingston, I'd consider it. But no. Not now, not ever.

"Rachel has a strict no fraternizing policy," I tell him before turning and walking to the elevator, not waiting for him. "Good night, Maverick," I say as I step into the elevator alone.

The morning comes way too quickly, and I'm rushing around trying to get dressed. I slept like shit, just because I never sleep well in hotels. My back is aching, and my head is killing me, so I pop two Tylenol and get ready. Rachel is expecting me to be at the airport early waiting for her arrival. If I'm not, I'm sure she'll rip my head off all the way back to the hotel. I hurry and call for my car, make a cup of shitty hotel coffee, then brush my teeth before making my way to the elevator.

It's barely seven in the morning, and the Texas heat punches me in the face as soon as I walk outside. The valet opens the door for me and hands me the keys, and I speed off toward the airport. The traffic is total shit, because it's the time most people head to work, and I start to panic when I realize I need to be at the airport within the next twenty minutes when her plane is scheduled to land. Granted, she has to go to baggage claim, but she's traveling with Angel, so she'll be extra cranky.

My heart races and I quickly take an exit trying to divert traffic, which was luckily the right decision. I circle around and wait for Rachel to come out, and as soon as I roll up, I start receiving texts from her. Yep, she's in a mood. I can already tell.

My heart drops when I realize I didn't get her a coffee before heading this way. As soon as I see her step out of the double doors, I hop out of the car and grab her suitcase as she holds Angel securely in her arms. The little devil in disguise has pink bows on her ears, and her diamond collar is sparkling in the sunshine. I'd offer to take the dog, but screw that. She'd bite my arm off.

I put on a smile. "How was the flight?"

She lifts her sunglasses and gives me a look. "The worst."

I open my mouth and close it. "I got keys for you to go ahead and check in to your room early. The hotel is really nice. I think you'll like it."

It takes every bit of strength I have to put her suitcases in the trunk. I laugh to myself, knowing it would never happen, but damn, I deserve a raise.

"Did you get me a coffee?" Rachel asks, glancing down at my cup.

"No, Starbucks was out of soy, so I told them never mind." It's a lie, but it's better than the truth.

She groans. "They need to get their crap together."

We pull out of the airport and drive back to the hotel.

"So remember, I need you to take care of Angel for me. She needs to go out every three hours, minimum. Also, she'll need food. I like to make sure there are no additives or fillers in it, and she's to only drink triple filtered bottled water. I don't want my baby to have any impurities from the tap." Rachel looks at Angel as if she's the most perfect creature on the planet.

I beg to differ.

Nodding, I do my best to control my face, though all I want to do is roll my eyes. I memorize everything she says, but we've already been through this. Her dog eats and drinks better than me.

As soon as we pull up to the hotel, the valet opens the door for Rachel, and she steps out, instantly replacing her scowl with a smile. She knows how to act, especially when she's staying in a hotel where her readers will be. *You never know who's watching you*, she always reminds me, which I know is good advice. Her bags are removed from the trunk, and the bellman offers to take them to her room. I hand over the key, and she hands me Angel, who instantly snaps at me.

"She might need to potty. Bring her to my room when she's finished."

Forcing another smile, I reply, "Of course."

I look down at Angel who's growling, showing all her pointy teeth. She's such a small dog, but damn, her bites hurt. I lead her to the grassy area and wait for her to smell almost every blade of grass there is, and when I'm totally annoyed, she waits another minute, then finally goes.

"I hate you," I say to her, and she turns around and flicks her back foot toward me as if to say the feeling is one hundred percent mutual.

"Okay, that's enough. Now you're just playing." I tug on her leash, and she snaps at me. I glare at her and pick the asshole up regardless of her aggravation. The entire way to the elevator, she acts out, and we can't get to the fifteenth floor soon enough. We step off, and I knock on Rachel's door, and she swings it open.

I step in and hand her off to Rachel who already has the doggy dishes set up in the room.

"So how's it been traveling with Maverick so far?" she asks, studying my face.

"A nightmare. We ran out of gas yesterday because he refused to fill up when I told him to."

She half-snorts before covering her mouth. "Doesn't surprise me. Even more reason for you to watch him tonight with my readers. I do not want to hear about him sleeping with any of them, Olivia. I'm very serious about that."

I nod. "It won't happen," I assure her. We quickly go over our schedule for tonight, and I pull all her clothes from her suitcase and hang them in the closet. I explain how I've already confirmed reservations at the hotel restaurant downstairs. "I'll be back around six to make sure you're ready. You're wearing a blue blouse and black skirt with these shoes," I tell her, showing her.

"Perfect. I'm going to get some writing done, then take a nap," she says.

"Room service is scheduled for noon," I remind her.

"Fantastic." She stands, and I take that as my cue to leave. Rachel doesn't have to say much anymore. I can read between the lines, and her body language gives her away every single time. Or maybe our brains have finally synced.

Instead of going back to my room and catching up on the sleep I desperately need, I run through the itinerary again. I go to the front desk and have them bring all the boxes of swag items we ordered for her readers to my room so I can put the gift bags together. We had fifty people confirmed for the meet-n-greet dinner. Rachel is graciously paying for everyone's food, though they have no idea yet.

Twenty minutes later, a bellman delivers six huge ass boxes to my room. I spend the next five hours putting everything together, and my back hurts even more from slouching and working a one-person assembly line.

After that's all done, I neatly pack the goody bags in three boxes, then make my way downstairs to the cafe to grab something quick to eat for lunch.

As soon as I walk in, I notice Maverick on his phone drinking a coffee in the corner. I pretend not to see him because I don't have the energy to deal with him right now. After I order a wrap and a bottle of water, I pay, grab my food, and walk out.

"Olivia." I hear a deep voice behind me and turn around to Maverick standing in front of me.

"Yes?" My stomach is growling, and all I want to do is swallow this wrap whole.

"What time tonight? Eight?" His smug smile tells me he's purposely trying to push my buttons. I'm exhausted, and my patience is hanging by a thread.

"Six. And I'm warning you right now, don't make me track you down," I tell him, bluntly shaking my head and walking to the elevators. I'm pretty sure I can hear his laughter echoing behind me.

After I eat and take a shower, I do some work on my laptop, then finally get dressed for the evening. Time passes by so quickly because when I look at the clock, it's time to go downstairs and make sure the room is set up correctly, or

Rachel will throw a fit. I call a bellman to bring a cart up for the boxes and deliver them to the reserved private room in the restaurant. As always, I feel like I'm rushing as I place the gift bags by each table setting. The bright pink tissue paper inside each bag perfectly matches Rachel's brand. After looking down at my watch to check the time, I hurry and go to Rachel's room and am pleasantly surprised when she's completely ready to go.

"I've already taken Angel out," she tells me and grabs her clutch. "Do I look okay?" She rubs her hands across her skirt. She's been stuck in the writing cave for so long, I haven't seen her in real clothes in months.

"You look perfect. Blue is your color. Ready to meet everyone?" I ask with a smile.

"I guess," she tells me, and I know she's nervous. Though she doesn't really like public events because she's an introvert, she's learned when she needs to put on an act. Rachel really does love meeting people who enjoy her words, though. That much I know is genuine.

We go downstairs, and as soon as she walks into the room, she's rushed by readers, and they surround her. The smile on her face is sincere as they discuss how much they love her characters and how excited they were about the release of the final book in her series. I look down at my watch and notice Maverick isn't anywhere around. We have fifteen minutes until the event officially begins, and he better pray to sweet baby Jesus that I don't have to hunt him down.

Thankfully, for him, he shows up right on time. The dinner goes well, and Rachel is in the spotlight. I try to keep off to the side, out of everyone's way and observe. Just as Rachel's readers are getting ready to leave, I see women crowd around Maverick, begging him for photos. He's being overly flirty and whispering in some of their ears. I watch as most of them undress him with their eyes, and he isn't doing himself any favors when he hugs them just a little too tightly. The numbers being exchanged isn't lost on me either.

When a woman decides to lift his shirt and place her hand on his abs, I walk across the room toward him. He's laughing, eating up all the attention. I pull him off to the side before his pants get torn off next.

"Best behavior," I tell him between gritted teeth. "I mean it."

"You need to chill out, babe. You've already got my number." He winks at me. Readers are calling him over, squealing over the wink and smile he flashes them as he tells them he'll be right back.

He takes me by surprise when he leans in, his lips softly brushing the shell of my ear. "If I didn't know better, I'd say you were jealous, Miss Priss."

My mouth falls open, and I'm two seconds from punching him in his abs of steel before he walks away, laughing.

CHAPTER EIGHT

MAVERICK

LAST NIGHT WAS MORE fun than I anticipated. It was a low-key chill dinner with Rachel's readers who asked her questions about the series and what she planned to write next. Olivia mostly observed, making sure the staff was doing their jobs and occasionally barking demands at me.

I know she keeps telling me to *behave*, but I'm not the one who starts the grabby hands game. When women act that way, I know they're just having fun and goofing off, so I don't ever feel the need to scold them. Especially last night when I was supposed to be "on the clock" and entertaining Rachel's fans. Seeing Olivia heated and annoyed was just the cherry on top.

After the evening was over, I spent an hour in the gym, then took a shower and went to bed. Today's the first signing, and I'm not quite sure how it all works. I've never been to an author event before, but Olivia keeps informing me of all the things I'm "expected" to do.

A knock sounds out, and when I look at my watch, I smile. Right on time. *As always.*

I wait a few moments before slowly walking to the door and unlocking it. Once I swing it open, I'm taken aback by the Olivia in front of me. She's dressed in her normal business attire, always so damn proper, except she's wearing knee-high boots over her dark pantyhose. Her skirt is tight, showing off every natural curve, and her top is pale pink. It's almost see-through, but I'm not going to mention that.

"Are you ready?" Her voice snaps me out of my haze, and I blink at her.

"Yeah, I just have to change."

Olivia's face drops as she scans my body. "What?"

"Relax," I say with a smile, then place my hands on her shoulders. "I'm kidding. But you're tense. You need a drink."

"It's ten in the morning," she says, her body slowly relaxing.

"I'm ready. Do I look okay for my first signing?" I take a step back so she can see what I'm wearing.

"Unless your shirt buttons to the inside of your jeans, I'm not sure it's going to stop them from lifting it again," she says, biting her lip and releasing a small laugh. It's cute.

"I guess I'll take my chances then." I smirk. "Gonna grab my wallet and phone real quick."

As soon as I have everything, Olivia and I walk to the elevator, and after she hits the button for the third floor, she turns and faces me. "Okay, so I started setting up a little this morning, but we need to go down and finish. All her preorders are organized, but I need help with the swag items. There are tote bags, plastic mason jars, pens, bookmarks, candles, and lip balms."

"Holy shit."

The elevator doors slide open, and I follow Olivia down a long hallway.

"Yeah, I had to ask for an extra table so she has room to sign. There's a bookseller on site so we won't have to worry about dealing with taking payments."

"This sounds way too complicated for just a signing." The moment the words come out of my mouth, we approach a hallway already filled with anxious readers. I stand stunned for a second as I realize this won't be anything like the intimate dinner we had last night.

"C'mon," Olivia says, grabbing my hand and dragging me behind her. "Keep moving forward or —"

"Oh my God, it's Ian!" one woman to my left yells, and it causes a ripple effect. Women shift in line and wave their arms around, screaming in pure excitement. I continue forward, flashing them grins, but keep walking like Olivia instructed.

The hallway seems to go on forever, the long line of people is never-ending, but we finally make it to the front of the line. Olivia rushes me inside to a massive ballroom where dozens of tables are set up in rows around the perimeter.

"You could've given me a heads-up!" I scold her as soon as we're in private.

She gives me a look and shakes her head. "I've been warning you for days! Last night was just a small taste of what you should expect."

"So I'm just supposed to stand around like a piece of eye candy? A slab of man meat? Their sex on a stick?"

"Okay, back up." Olivia bursts out laughing. "I figured you'd like having your ego stroked, so what's the problem?"

"There's no problem," I quickly say. "I can take pictures and smile pretty."

She snorts, handing me a box. "You're basically an expert

at that. Now place those mason jars on that table over there. Make sure her name and logo are facing out."

"So...how crazy are these readers?" I quietly ask Olivia about an hour after everything's set up. "Do I need pepper spray?" I half-joke.

"They aren't crazy. They're just...passionate. Rachel's readers are obsessed with the Bayshore Coast *series*, and you're the representation of the hero. They basically put you on a pedestal and bow down to you because of her character. For them, meeting you is the closest way to feel connected to Rachel's series, which is why so many of them like getting your autograph and taking pictures with you. It feels special to them, and it's something they will always cherish. So that's what you're doing here. This series means a lot to many of her readers for various reasons. Sometimes it's the emotional aspects, the funny moments, the family history, but Ian is who they ultimately fall for and root for throughout."

"Wow...that's the sincerest thing I've ever heard you say without disdain or disgust. Passionate and obsessed, that's how you are with your job." She gives me a look. "In a good way," I add. "But okay, I think I get it now. Channeling my inner Ian."

She smiles, then laughs. "Yes, which should be easy for you, considering Ian was a classic asshole. Arrogant, wealthy, full of himself."

"Women falling to their knees, begging for just one night," I add for her with a cocky grin.

Olivia rolls her eyes right on cue. "Focus, Maverick. Be polite, warming, and welcoming, offer to take pictures — some get too nervous to ask — sign their books or swag, and thank them for coming. Tell them it was a pleasure to meet them and move to the next person waiting to meet you, treating them each like they were the first reader in line."

"Like a pimp assembly line." I smirk.

Olivia groans, shaking her head. "Let's finish up, *Pimp Daddy.*" I can tell she's holding back a smile, which I find amusing.

She turns around, and as she's fiddling with something, I stand behind her and press my chest to her back. The moment I lean in and my mouth closes in on her ear, her body tenses. "You can call me Daddy anytime, sweetheart." She shivers, though I know she'd never admit it. Her body reacts when mine is close, and I take that as a small victory.

An emcee interrupts our moment, and Olivia jumps, which puts space between us. The announcer lets everyone know the VIP ticket session is starting soon and the author photo will be in twenty minutes.

"Shit, Rachel better get here." She types away on her phone seconds later. "Lord knows I can't leave you here by yourself…"

And just like that, our special moment is gone.

"I'm a big boy, ya know? If you need to go check on her, I'll be fine."

Turning and looking at me, she contemplates my suggestion. She opens her mouth, but then her phone goes off, and she starts typing away again.

"She's ready. I'm going to meet her at the elevators. Be right back." Olivia takes a couple of steps forward, then stops to face me. "I didn't mean to imply you couldn't be here by yourself because I didn't trust *you*, but things are about to get really chaotic with eight hundred people in one room. You're my responsibility, and I just want to make sure you don't get bombarded or overwhelmed or kidnapped."

And there's another layer shredded off Olivia Carpenter. Damn. She almost sounds sincere.

I nearly close the gap between us. She tilts her head to look up at me, and while my eyes lock with hers, I grab her arms and softly squeeze. "I'll be fine, okay? Everything's going to be great. Stop worrying. You've got this."

Olivia looks at me as if she's never heard words of encouragement before. "Right." She nods, almost stunned. "Thanks."

After the authors huddle together and take a group photo, the room is buzzing with VIP ticket holders dragging their big ass carts and wagons behind them. People are waiting in long lines, squealing over their favorite authors and shouting in excitement. It's like a Black Friday sale for book lovers.

So far, I've taken pictures with Rachel at her table for readers and also stood and took some selfies with them. Rachel doesn't get up for photos, so they have to come behind the table and pose with her. I kinda don't blame her since she'd be getting up and down every five seconds, but I'd rather just stay standing at this point.

"The doors are about to open for the rest of the ticket holders," Olivia warns.

"There's *more* coming in?"

She chuckles slightly. "Yep. A lot more. So hold on to your shirt."

Rachel looks back and forth between Olivia and me, and I wonder what she's thinking. She's not said much to me since she arrived. Pleasant and kind, but just not with many words.

"I hope Olivia reminded you of the rules and expectations." Rachel speaks to me slowly, enunciating each word as though I'm incapable of understanding her.

"Of course she has. I'm well versed on what the expectations are," I say firmly.

"Good." Rachel turns to Olivia next. "I'll need another coffee."

Olivia looks at her watch and scrambles to her feet. "Of course."

"Don't you want to ask if Maverick needs anything? He's working hard today too." Rachel puts her on the spot, and if the space between us didn't feel tense and awkward, I'd be tempted to burst out laughing at Olivia's shell-shocked face at the implication that she's *not* working hard. It was a low blow because after a few days with Olivia, I know she busts her ass for that woman.

"Maverick," Olivia says slowly, swallowing as if waiting on me is physically painful for her. It makes me smile. "Can I get you anything to drink?"

"As a matter of fact, I'm kinda feeling a beer. Think you can get that for me, sweetheart?" I shoot her a wink only because I know it'll drive her crazy—and not in a good way.

"You shouldn't be drinking during the event. It's unprofessional," she tells me, crossing her arms, growing more impatient with me.

"Olivia," Rachel snaps, and Olivia instantly stands taller. "You'll get Maverick whatever he asks for. He's my guest of honor, and he'll be treated as such."

Olivia forces a smile and turns toward me. I smirk, because it's one small victory, though I know she'll ream out my ass for this later.

"Of course. I'll be right back." She grits her teeth and

narrows her eyes at me. If looks could kill, holy fuck — Olivia would have buried me six feet under.

Most women would be more than happy to get me whatever I ask for, but not Miss Priss. No, she thrives on hating me and bossing me around. Not that I don't kind of like it, but I can't help but wonder why she loathes me so much. It has to be something on a deeper level than just my so-called reputation.

And I have eight days to figure out what it is.

CHAPTER NINE

OLIVIA

I LOVE MY JOB. I love my job. I love my job.

Maybe if I say it over and over in my head, I'll actually convince myself this isn't the most humiliating job right now. I love it most days, but this trip has definitely stretched me thin, and it's only the first city stop on the tour.

Lord help me.

After grabbing Rachel's coffee from the hotel cafe, I rush to the other side of the bar and order a bottle of Bud Light. There weren't many options, so Maverick better take it and love it.

By the time I make it back down to the ballroom, readers are being let in, and now I'm rushing through them to get back to Rachel's table before all hell breaks loose.

"What took you so long?" Rachel snaps, snatching her coffee out of my hand and taking a long swig. "The line is forming and blocking the walkway."

"I'll take care of it," I tell her, handing Maverick his beer. I hear a faint, *"Thank you,"* but I don't have time to reply because Rachel's right. Her line has reached across the walk-through area, and I need to get them moved over.

"Hey, guys! Can I just ask that you please all shift a tad over here so we aren't blocking people or the other tables in?" I say loudly and cheerfully, directing them where to move. I know the event has volunteers who are supposed to help with this kind of stuff, but since the doors just opened, everything is hectic. "Thank you so much." I smile at them. "Don't forget to grab your books from the bookseller, and Rachel and Ian would love to sign them for you!" At the mention of *Ian*, readers start squealing all over again.

Most of Rachel's readers brought their own copies for her to sign. I can see them stacked high in their arms and carts. Since the last book in the series just released, they're eager to get them all signed by both of them.

Once the line shifts, I motion for the readers to start coming up, and as Rachel kindly greets each one, Maverick stands and gives them hugs and poses for selfies. They both make small talk with each reader, and even though the line seems never-ending, they handle it flawlessly.

Maverick is sweet and charming and really plays his part as Ian. Some of the younger women asked for group shots, so of course, I played photographer, and after snapping a couple of good ones, one girl yells out, "Silly pic now!" They all giggle and stick their tongues out; however, the one closest to Maverick actually swipes her tongue on his face and licks his cheek. Maverick's in a rocker pose with his tongue out and his hands in a rock-on sign. I snap the picture, and it's actually kinda cute, minus the cheek-licker.

"I feel like I need to bathe in sanitizer after all this." Maverick leans over and whispers in my ear when things start to slow down a tad.

"For your sake, you actually should," I fire back playfully. "That one girl probably gave you herpes of the cheek or something."

Maverick's head falls back as he bellows out a loud laugh. "Yeah, I didn't see that coming, but at least I didn't turn my head at that exact time. Would've turned things straight into Rated R territory." He winks as if that makes what he said any better. I pretend to retch at his implication and make a gagging noise.

The signing comes to an end, and although it was very successful for Rachel, I'm exhausted and ready to lay low the rest of the night. She has a dinner meeting in about an hour, which means after I take care of Angel, I'll finally get the night to myself.

"Do you need me to get you anything before you leave tonight?" I ask Rachel as she grabs her bag and stands. The signing has ended, and people are now just scrambling to clean up their tables.

"No, I'll manage just fine."

Rachel walks out without another word, and I'm left to deal with the aftermath of picking up her leftover swag bags and banners. I'm kneeling on the floor, packing up, and meanwhile, Maverick is surrounded by a crowd of women — no shocker there — but then I hear one of them invite him out to a bar tonight to eat and get drinks. I crane my neck to get a better look at who he's talking to, and I see it's a group of readers and a couple of authors.

Going out with them while being under Rachel's thumb is the exact scenario of what not to do, and he should know better too. But then I hear the idiot tell them he'd love to meet up with them.

Son of a bitch.

"Maverick." I say his name flatly, trying to grab his attention while making sure I remain professional around the group of people. "I could use your assistance, please, to get these boxes out of here."

A round of sad aww's linger at his departure, but he reassures them he'll be seeing them in the bar later.

"Just this box here?" he asks while I keep my head down, pretending to focus on the filthy floor I'm sitting on.

"Yeah, and those two banners." I nod my head toward the table behind him where I set them down and put them in their bags.

"Olivia."

His deep, firm voice forces me to look up at him. "What?"

"What are you doing?" He crosses his arms, looking confused.

"I'm picking up the mess I made with the tissue paper from the swag bags."

"You know they probably have a cleaning crew for after these big events. You picking up teeny tiny pieces of paper is doing nothing to help."

I look around and know he's right. I just needed a distraction from the fact all the attention he was getting from those women *annoyed* me, which in and of itself is annoying that it bothers me. This whole damn trip is annoying.

Lifting myself to my feet, I grab my bag and the second swag box and instruct him to grab the rest so we can get out of here before another tribe of women tackle him—except I leave that last part out.

"I just need to drop these off at my room quick then take out the devil dog," I tell him as we ride the elevator to my floor.

"The devil dog?" He pops a brow.

"Rachel's dog, *Angel*. She hates me and tries to bite me every chance she gets."

Maverick chuckles and shakes his head.

"How is that funny? She's a real terror!"

"She can probably smell fear and stress."

"I do not smell like fear and stress," I counter, scrunching my nose. "She's just an evil little shit."

Maverick walks behind me as I lead us to my room, and once we're inside, we drop off the boxes and banners. I sent a bunch of swag bags to each of the event hotels, so we'll take these with us as extras, just in case.

The moment I turn around, I walk smack into Maverick's chest, not realizing how close he was to me still. "Geez, boundaries." I snicker.

"You're the one who invited me into your room." He smirks, holding my shoulders with his large hands. Big and sturdy. *Oh God*. Not going there.

Not wanting him to see the blush creeping over my cheeks, I playfully smack him and laugh. "I did not invite you into my room. Why do you take everything so literal? I asked you to help me drop off the boxes so you wouldn't get swept away by that group of readers."

He steps back slightly, studying me. "You really gonna tell me I can't go hang out at the bar with some of the fans? Plus, I'm starving and need to eat. What's the harm?"

"That's exactly what I'm saying. And the harm is, it's not professional. They were already all over you, so you think having alcohol in their systems is going to help?"

"Well, if you're so worried, why don't you come chaperone then?"

He really is going to push every single button of mine before this trip is over.

"I don't have time to argue with you. I need to take care of Rachel's stupid dog." I grab my bag so I can march out of there with my head held high, but of course, Maverick never makes anything easy on me.

"Okay, I'll meet you down there then," he shouts after me. I give him a one-finger wave over my shoulder before the door shuts behind me.

Thirty minutes later, I'm standing outside waiting for a ten-pound dog to finally take a shit so I can get to the bar and make sure Maverick behaves.

Ugh! I just wanted a quiet, relaxing night, and now I have to eat dinner in a noisy bar while keeping an eye on the hands of every woman who gets within a foot of Maverick.

"I will pay you a hundred dollars to just pick a damn spot, Angel!" I whisper-shout at her. "Think of all the amazing toys and bones you can buy with that? C'mon, just help a girl out!" Apparently, I'm not above begging a dog who has no idea what I'm even saying.

Ten minutes later, she's happy as can be and wagging her tail now that she's relieved herself. "It's about damn time." I pout, walking her back to Rachel's room. I bring her inside and lock the door behind me. Just as I'm about to get on the elevator and head to the bar, I decide to go back to my room and freshen up first.

I change into another outfit, something a bit dressier for night. I brush through my hair and dab more powder on my face. I don't even know why I care at this point, but I tell myself it's because even though Rachel has essentially given us the night off, people around the hotel could still recognize me as her assistant.

I make it down to the bar, and of course, it's already packed and loud with drunk people. At this point, I'm too hungry to care and weasel my way through the crowd. Just as I ask for a food menu from the bartender, a seat opens up, and I quickly take it.

"What can I get for you, darlin'?" a male bartender asks in a super friendly tone, and I'm convinced it's just the Southern culture.

"I'd like a glass of Chardonnay and the shrimp fettuccine alfredo with a Caesar salad, please."

"Of course. I'll go put your order in and be right back with your drink."

"Great, thank you."

I quickly scan the room for Maverick, wondering if he's actually down here. Just when I'm about to give up looking for him, I hear a bunch of ladies in the back scream-laugh and causing a commotion.

Looking over my shoulder, I finally spot him in a circle of women—*no surprise*—and they're all flashing him googly eyes.

Like he needs his ego stroked any more, ladies.

I mean, I see the appeal. I really do. He's the full package that most girls go crazy over, and if we had met under different circumstances, I might even say he has a decent personality. But even then, he's the exact type I stay away from.

My drink arrives, and I slowly sip it, only looking over my shoulder to check on Maverick a couple more times. I actually do trust that he will behave, but I don't always trust he'll know how to react if *they* don't behave.

Finally, my food arrives, and I don't hesitate to dig right in. About halfway through my pasta dish, I hear my name being called and look over my shoulder to Maverick waving me over.

"Join us," he shouts over the crowd, which causes me to blush with embarrassment. "They're telling me all about the dirty books you guys read." The ladies giggle and scoot closer to him. It makes me cringe.

I'm not about to yell in a bar and have a conversation, so I lift my salad bowl up and mouth, *"I'm eating."*

"Oh come on!" he shouts again, this time even louder.

I force a smile and shake my head before turning back around. Looking up from my food, I immediately see the bartender standing in front of me.

"How is everything? Need a refill?" he asks, holding up my empty wineglass.

"Uh, sure, why not? Thanks!"

"You got it." He shoots me a wink, then pulls the bottle out and pours me another glass. "There you go, darlin'."

"Thank you."

"Either that pasta is giving you the best orgasm of your life, or you're just really hungry." Maverick's voice rings in my ear as he stands next to me. "I heard you moaning from all the way over there."

I quickly swallow and glance at his smug expression. "Are you sure you weren't hearing one of your groupies moaning for your attention?"

"You're sure hung up on who I hang out with."

I stare into his eyes and narrow mine, so he gets my message loud and clear. "It's my job, Maverick. Remember?"

"You're off the clock, Olivia. You're down here checking on me, *by choice*," he retorts, taking the seat next to me. I look over my shoulder to see his group is still there, obviously waiting for him to return. "I told them I had another fan to give my attention to," he says when he catches me looking at them.

His answer makes me laugh sarcastically. "A fan? That's a bit far-fetched."

"Oh come on. You said yourself you like this Ian character. So just pretend I'm him," he retorts with a stupid smile on his gorgeous face.

"If you knew me at all, you'd know you're preaching to the wrong choir."

"And why's that? Prefer the vagina?"

"Maverick!" I scold around a mouthful of food. His bold statement is forcing me to hold back laughter. Once I swallow it down and compose myself, I shoot him a disapproving look. "Do you just say the first thing that pops into your brain?"

"Well, no...not the first thing." He smirks with a playful shrug. "I mean, no judgment on my part. I'm a huge fan of vagina myself."

"Oookay, we're still on that. Just because I don't throw myself at you doesn't mean I'm a lesbian."

"I never said that. I only suggested it after you said I was preaching to the wrong choir."

"Meaning, I don't go gaga over book boyfriends and models. It's just not my...thing. I appreciate them, and I love reading about them, but I don't give myself a lot of time to dwell over the fantasy of the *perfect guy*. He doesn't exist, so I focus on my own life."

"You mean, *controlling* every aspect of it," he counters, leaning over to swipe a piece of my shrimp.

"Manners!" I swat at his hand, but it's too late. He shoves it into his mouth before I can stop him.

"I like having control. I don't feel the need to live a carefree, wild life. I don't judge others who prefer to live a different lifestyle than me either, so I expect the same respect in return," I say matter-of-factly.

"And where does that stem from?"

"What do you mean?"

"The need to control everything. I assume you didn't come out of the womb screaming for your planner bible."

That makes me chuckle, and I shake my head at him. "No, but I did appreciate being on a consistent schedule as a kid. I thrived on it." I find myself thinking about my childhood and force the thoughts away. Not right now.

"You need to learn to let go and live a little," he leans in and whispers softly. "You're going to wake up one day and realize that trying to control everything all the time isn't really living."

My mouth opens to disagree with him, but nothing comes to mind, so I clamp it shut.

"You think on that for a while." He shoots me a wink and pushes himself off the chair.

Fifteen minutes later, I'm still thinking about what Maverick said, and allowing his words to eat at me is frustrating. I finish my third glass of wine and wave at the bartender for my check.

"You're all paid up, ma'am." He sets down the receipt with Maverick's handwriting scribbled at the bottom.

What the hell? When did he do that? And why?

I reach for my phone and quickly send him a text.

Olivia: You didn't have to pay for my food. But thank you.

Maverick: A man should always pay. And you're welcome.

Olivia: That only applies during a date. We weren't on a date.

Maverick: I beg to differ. There was food, wine, good conversation. Best date I've ever been on.

His message makes me blush for real now. Who the hell is *this* guy?

Olivia: You're delusional. I'm going to bed now. We have that brunch in the morning.

Maverick: I'll walk with you. Stay right there.

Just as I'm about to tell him it's not necessary, I hear him telling the ladies good night and that it was a pleasure meeting and talking with them. Given the fact he didn't even have to be "on the clock" tonight, he sure made a lot of people happy.

"Ready?" he asks as soon as he's next to me, taking my hand and pulling me up from the chair. "You're a light-weight, aren't you?" He chuckles, tightening his grip on me.

"No. I'm fine. It's just these stupid barstools are hard to get out of."

I finally manage to land on my feet and look up to see Maverick smiling at me. "What?"

"I think I like tipsy Olivia. She's right up there with all-natural Olivia. I think I like her the most."

We walk toward the elevators. "What are you talking about?"

"Your different personalities. There's uptight Olivia—aka Miss Priss—then there's the Olivia under all those work clothes and makeup—all-natural Olivia—and now there's happy-go-lucky, tipsy Olivia."

I turn to face him as we wait for the elevator. "And what are your personalities, Maverick? You put this act on like you're this carefree, give-no-shits surfer boy, but that can't be all there is to you, is there?"

The doors swing open, and Maverick puts his hand on the small of my back to give me a small push to walk through. I watch as he hits the button for my floor.

"Also, you know what's really been chapping my ass?" I turn toward him again, and he's chuckling. "Why the hell don't you fly? Don't you know it's actually safer than driving? It can be a tad scary during turbulence, but the fly time is like a millisecond compared to the driving time." I can't help the word vomit spewing out of my mouth, but as soon as I look up and see Maverick's face, I regret it.

His face has dropped, his eyes low, and his shoulders slumped over.

"I think I should get you to bed if you're going to be on time for brunch in the morning." The doors open moments later, and he guides me out again and walks me to my room. I fiddle with the key, but the damn thing won't scan.

"Let me try." Maverick pulls a key out from his wallet and effortlessly opens the door.

"Wait. How'd you do that? Why do you have a key to my room?"

"Just a precautionary." He winks at me, but it's with a frown over his face.

"I'll be fine," I tell him, though I'm mostly trying to convince myself. "Brunch is at eleven. Don't be late."

"I know the drill." He smirks. "Good night, Olivia."

I look up and see him watching me. "Night." And for a split second, I almost ask him to stay.

CHAPTER TEN

MAVERICK

IF I'M BEING TRUTHFUL, I wasn't looking forward to this trip. I didn't know what to expect, considering I've never toured with an author before, but so far, it's been pretty cool. This morning, we had a brunch with Rachel's readers, and while many of them focused on asking her questions, others were too busy handing me their phone numbers. At this point, I'm pretty sure I have so many, I could use them like confetti. And yes, I know the rules. I don't plan on getting with any of them, but it's fun to watch Olivia squirm, just like she's doing right now.

One of Rachel's readers keeps leaning over and placing her hand on my thigh. She's beautiful but not my type. Then again, if I weren't on this tour, I'd probably go back to her room with her and show her a good time. Especially since she's throwing out all the signals. I know exactly what she wants, and by the look on Olivia's face, she knows too.

After the brunch is over, I'm standing around waiting for Rachel. A reader comes to me, talking too close, and Olivia smiles at the woman, thanks her for coming, then pulls me away.

"Your middle name should be Cockblock," I say as she pulls me onto the elevator and presses my floor along with hers since we're on different levels.

Her mouth is tight in a firm line. "We're leaving in thirty minutes. We need to make it to Amarillo before dark. I have a lot of work to do."

The elevator stops on her floor, and she steps out. Before the doors close, she turns around and looks at me. "Do not be late."

And that warning is the reason I purposely take my time packing my things. I wish Olivia would stop with the act because I can see straight through it, though she'd never admit it. She's too concerned with her image to let her hair down and relax every once in a while. I can't imagine not ever being off the clock. Life isn't that serious or shouldn't be taken that way.

After I go to my room and get my stuff together, I wait until I'm supposed to be downstairs, then head toward the elevator, making sure not to rush. By the time I'm on the ground floor, Olivia is already in the car waiting. She pops the trunk, and I throw my suitcase inside, then climb into the passenger seat.

"You did that on purpose," she says, punching on the gas and pulling out of the parking lot. She gets up on the highway and drives through the city like she's a native or a maniac.

"You'll eventually learn I only need to be told to be somewhere one time," I tell her.

Once we're out of Dallas, she slightly relaxes. Something's streaming between us, and it's awkward. I don't really know what to say, and it shocks me that I'm tongue-tied for words. She sings along to an annoying pop song on the radio, and I laugh.

"Is this Justin Bieber?" I look down at the title on the screen to confirm.

"I love the Biebs," she tells me with a smile, going back to her lyrics.

I shake my head. "Don't you ever admit that in public."

"I like other music too. Especially the eighties and nineties. But my guilty pleasure is pop music and Taylor Swift."

"I'm trying really hard not to judge you right now." I grin.

We make small talk, and when we stop for gas, we switch places, and I drive the rest of the way. We're making good time, and I'm thankful no disaster has happened today. We got off to a bad start, but I think Olivia is beginning to soften up to me, or maybe my mind is playing tricks on me. I glance over at her while she works, and we exchange small innocent smiles before she goes back to scribbling in her notebook.

The GPS directs me to take the next exit, so I pull off the highway and travel down a few miles until we're pulling up to our hotel. We pull up to the valet, and I grab our suitcases. I stand back while Olivia checks in, which is taking much longer than it usually does. I walk up to the counter and stand next to her.

"Can you check again and make sure?" Olivia asks the woman in a panicked tone. She types on the computer then looks up.

"I'm sorry, Ms. Carpenter. We only have one room available for you."

I glance over at Olivia who's about to blow smoke out of her ears, she's so noticeably pissed.

"The hotel was overbooked. We tried to call you earlier this week to let you know there was an issue with your reservation, and one of them was being canceled so other arrangements could be made."

Olivia huffs. "I didn't get a call. My service has been in and out while I've been traveling."

"One room should be fine," I tell the woman with a smile. She instantly smiles back at me.

Olivia rolls her eyes. "I guess it will *have* to be."

The woman apologizes again, then explains where the elevators are and what time breakfast will be served. I take the key cards, wink at the receptionist, and then the two of us walk away. Olivia is raging, and I actually find it cute.

"I'm so livid," she seethes as we step on the elevator. "The review I'm leaving for this hotel…"

"It's only for one night," I remind her. "What could happen?"

She glances over at me. I give her a smirk, and she groans.

"Don't be nervous. I don't bite. Too hard." I chuckle as the elevator doors slide open.

Olivia leads the way to the room, and I study her from behind.

"I can only imagine the cheesy pickup lines you use on women," she says. "This is why I read so many romance books."

She swipes the card across the sensor, and the door clicks open.

"Reading those kind of romances can set unrealistic

expectations in a relationship," I tell her, locking the door behind us.

With one swift movement, she throws her suitcase and laptop bag on the edge of the mattress. "Great, one bed," she says to herself, groaning. "Or maybe it just sets the bar higher? When I do decide to get in a serious relationship, it's not going to be with just any man who can whisper sweet nothings in my ear. He'll have to be someone special, someone worth my time. Otherwise, I'm happy with how things are right now." She digs into her bag and pulls out some clothes. "Do you need to go to the restroom? I'm going to take a shower."

"Olivia, that man exists out there. And when you find him, you'll know. And no, I'm good. I'm probably gonna go work out. My muscles are stiff from sitting so long," I tell her before she walks into the bathroom.

She gives me a look, almost as if she's contemplating my words before walking to the bathroom. Something streams between us, but I try to ignore it, though it's hard. Once the door is locked and the water is running, I quickly change into some shorts and a dry-fit shirt, grab my headphones from my bag, and head to the gym.

Once I'm there, I do a few warm-up reps with the bar before I start adding heavy weights. I'm trying to focus, but I'm finding it a bit hard, and the only person to blame is Olivia. Though she's a prude and uptight and gets on my nerves more often than not, I can't help but be intrigued by her. It's refreshing how she doesn't fall at my feet. For the first time in a long while, I have someone determined to challenge me at every corner, and I kinda like it. Shaking the thoughts of her out of my head, I push myself to the limit. Once I've completed my reps, I make my way back to the room. As soon as I walk in, I can smell the sweetness of her shampoo and body wash.

I continue forward and am almost taken aback when I see her sitting with her legs crossed and laptop on the bed. Her wet hair is down, black-framed glasses on her face, and she's wearing a T-shirt and pajama bottoms. My mouth falls open, and I hurry to try to close it.

"Hi. My name is Maverick Kingston, and you are?" I hold my hand out to reintroduce myself to this stranger in my room. I'm not sure what I expected to find when I came back, but it wasn't Olivia looking so...normal. It's hot.

She swats at my hand and laughs. "Shut up, Maverick!" She dramatically rolls her eyes at me, then goes back to her computer.

I'm trying not to stare, but damn, it's so hard when she looks so naturally beautiful. Instead of standing there gawking, I force myself to go to the bathroom and run the water. Considering I'm sweaty as hell and need a distraction, I take a shower. Once I'm out of my clothes, I turn the water as hot as I can stand it and step in. The warmth feels good against my sore muscles, and I try to enjoy it, considering I've been sitting for most of the day. After my skin is pruned, I force myself to get out, and that's when I realize I didn't grab any clothes.

Shit. I'm used to staying in a room by myself, but I use this as the perfect opportunity to make Olivia squirm. I quietly chuckle just thinking about it as I finish drying off and wrap the towel around my waist, then walk into the bedroom.

I try to pretend as if I don't notice Olivia looking over her laptop at me. It gives me a rush, knowing her eyes are on my body. I make eye contact with her and lift an eyebrow as

I reach for my suitcase, and that's when my towel falls from my waist into a pool on the floor. Instead of trying to hide, I just go with it. Olivia's eyes go wide as she checks out the full package, then her mouth falls open, which only causes me to smirk. I'm not a shy guy or embarrassed because I have a lot to be proud of.

"Maverick! Put on some clothes! Oh my God!" She picks up a pillow and throws it at me before covering her eyes.

I shrug, and dig out some pajama pants and slip them on. "Sorry, that was an accident."

She moves her hand from her face and glares at me. "I really doubt that. You were way too confident standing there. I mean, if you wanted to show off your dick, you could've asked first."

Laughter tumbles out of me. "Yeah right. You seem way too modest for that."

"I didn't say I'd say yes. Let me be very clear, I would've said hell no."

I nod at her. "Right. You're telling me you weren't even curious?"

When I sit on the other side of the bed, Olivia instantly stands. "Nope. No. No way. Totally inappropriate."

I snort. Always the professional. "Have you even seen a dick in real life before? You looked as if it was going to bite you." I know I'm crossing a line, but I can't help it. She's adorable when she gets all flustered.

"Probably does bite. Has to fight off all the women scrambling to jump on it."

I look at her, stunned.

"Shit, sorry. That was rude. You probably have a fine, satisfying dick. I just wasn't interested in seeing it."

Her words have my chest shaking with laughter. Not only is she as uptight as she looks on most days, but she's also socially awkward as hell. Though I actually find it refreshing.

"No worries. I've never had any complaints before." I grab my phone off the nightstand and start scrolling through my apps. When she doesn't sit back down, I glance over at her. Messy blond hair, glasses, wearing a baggy T-shirt with a coffee cup on it. She's stunning without her business costume on. It's the first time I've really seen her let her hair down, and there's an internal shift I can't deny. I swallow hard and look at her. "What?"

"We have to have some rules tonight," she tells me, but I can see the blush on her cheeks. Is it possible that I've broken through, made her nervous as hell? If so, mission accomplished.

"I'd expect nothing less, honestly."

She scoffs. "First, you need to put a shirt on too. The pants aren't enough."

I stand. "I work really hard for these abs." Yep, now she's staring.

She moves around the bed. "And we need a pillow wall between us when we go to sleep."

Now I'm laughing. "Why?"

"Because. I'm actually afraid of the anaconda in your pants."

Her words cause me to double over. "Anaconda? Well, I think you're safe. He doesn't just let himself out in the middle of the night and search for single women."

"You sure about that?" She lifts an eyebrow.

"Wow. You've got jokes. That's a first," I throw back at her. "Trust me when I say I have no intentions of crossing the invisible line you've already drawn on the bed. I'll stick to my side, and you stick to yours. Unless you change your mind." I shoot her a wink.

In one swift movement, she picks up another pillow and chucks it at me as hard as she can. She's smiling and laughing, and she's finally releasing all the weight she carries around on her shoulders. This is the Olivia I want to get to know. Not the woman who wears tight skirts and button-up collared shirts. That version of her doesn't know how to have a good time or break out of a schedule. But the woman standing in front of me is someone totally different.

I smile at her. "I'm actually going to go to bed, I think. I'm exhausted."

"What about the rules?" she asks, sitting back on the bed.

Pulling the blankets down, I slip between the sheets. "If you learn one thing before this trip is over, Olivia, it's that I don't play by the rules."

I roll over on my side, where my back is toward her, and click off the lamp on the table. "Good night, Miss Priss," I tell her before I close my eyes.

"Good night, Mr. Playboy," she retorts, but I can tell she's smiling.

CHAPTER ELEVEN

OLIVIA

As soon as my alarm goes off, I peel my eyes open. For a moment, I have no idea where I am, then I remember I'm in a hotel room with Maverick. Carefully, I slide out of bed and stand only to realize he's not here. I let out a deep breath and walk to the bathroom for my morning routine.

I'm surprised I got any sleep at all, considering each time I closed my eyes, all I could see was Maverick standing so confident, showing off his goods. Damn, that man is poison. With everything I have, I try to shake the image from my mind, but it's inconveniently plastered there.

After I wash my face and brush my teeth, I pack up my things because we'll need to leave soon. I stuff my toiletries in the suitcase and pull out my clothes for the day. After I've changed, Maverick walks through the door, sweating. I try not to make eye contact or stare as he pulls his shirt over his head.

"Mornin'," he says with a shit-eating grin plastered on his face.

I narrow my eyes at him, trying to keep my gaze above his chest. "What?"

"Did you sleep okay?" He's still smiling as he walks to his suitcase and pulls out a change of clothes.

"I did, why?" He's making me really suspicious by how weird he's acting, and considering I haven't had a drop of coffee yet, I'm not in the mood for his games.

"Has anyone ever told you how much you talk in your sleep?"

My heart begins to race, and my mouth goes dry. "What did I say?"

There's that panty-melting smirk again, and that's all he leaves me with before he goes into the bathroom and shuts the door. The water comes on, and I stand there holding my chest, trying to remember any of the dreams I had last night, but I'm drawing a blank. What the hell did I say? He's probably just fucking with me...right?

Instead of dwelling on it, I call a valet to have the car moved around. I knock on the bathroom door to let him know my plans before I leave.

"I'm going down to the car. You have ten minutes before I leave without you," I tell him, and all he does is laugh.

Shaking my head, I grab my stuff and head to the lobby, still trying to figure out what the hell I could've said in my sleep. Before the day's over, I will get it out of him, or it will be his ass.

When I walk outside, the car is parked and waiting for me. An older gentleman places my suitcases in the trunk and opens the driver's door. Considering how much they weigh, I tip him well. He thanks me, and I pull up to make more room for other cars as I wait for Maverick. Ten minutes pass and I'm so close to going back to the room and dragging him down here, but then I think maybe I'll just drive off to teach him a lesson. Just as I'm contemplating my options, he comes waltzing out of the double doors with a pep in his step. I pop the trunk, and he throws his suitcase in, then walks around to my side.

"I'm driving first," he bends down and says.

I shake my head. "Get in the damn car."

Crossing his arms over his broad chest, he just stands there. We should've already been on the road, so instead of arguing with him, I get out and switch places.

"See how easy it is when you listen to me." He flashes a victorious grin as we buckle our seat belts.

"Why are you looking at me like that?" I finally ask as I pull my laptop out of my bag and connect it to my hotspot.

He shrugs.

"Just tell me what I said. You're starting to irritate me." I huff.

Licking his lips, he sucks in a deep breath. I wait impatiently for him to speak, but he's taking his sweet time. "It's nothing really. You were just moaning my name over and over and *over* again."

My mouth drops open. "No, I wasn't. You're so lying right now."

Maverick chuckles. "Okay then. I may or may not have a video of it. It was dark, but I could tell by the tone of your voice that you were enjoying it. Must've been a really great dream although, if you ask me, real life is *much* better."

"I swear on your career, Maverick, if you recorded me, I'll—"

"Maybe I'll accidentally text it to Rachel and see what she has to say about it," he interrupts.

A groan releases from my throat. "You're determined to drive me crazy."

"Only six more days to make that happen. Though to be fair, I think you were already a little crazy."

I glare at him, but it doesn't faze him in the least. He turns on some music and goes into his little world, just as I go into mine. For an hour, I reply to emails regarding Rachel's next book release. Though we're still celebrating the grand finale of the Bayshore Coast series, Rachel is always a few books ahead, which means I never get a real break.

I've been texting my old boss, Vada, during this trip and giving her updates. When she first heard about Rachel forcing me to road trip with Maverick, she laughed her ass off—at my expense, of course. Then she begged me to give her all the juicy details so she could put it in a book.

Now every day she asks me for updates.

Vada: So, big? Or BIG BIG? :)

I hold back a chuckle because I don't want Maverick to know I'm texting about him.

Olivia: Why are you so interested in another man's dick? Don't think Ethan would approve.

Vada: Are you kidding me? He's asking for more details than I am, and it's much worse! We're both quite invested and are placing bets.

Olivia: Placing bets on what?

Vada: ...er, nothing. Never mind.

Olivia: VADA!! You better tell me, or I'm not giving you any more info.

Vada: You wouldn't do that to me! :'(

Olivia: ...try me.

Vada: Gah! I forget how good you are at playing hardball. Fine! We placed a bet on how long until you two finally sleep together.

Olivia: OMG! Why would you bet that? Whoever placed that bet is going to LOSE!

Vada: So, he's small then? :(

I swallow down a laugh, though imagining her voice in my head is enough to send me over the edge and blow my cover. She was always such an introvert, all business and obsessed with her cat, Oliver. Now she's going to Saturday morning farmers' markets with her husband and new baby, London. Vada's a whole different person from when we first met, but regardless, I'm super happy for her. Her entire demeanor has changed, and I know she's the happiest she's ever been in her life.

Vada: Hey, Liv. It's Ethan. I've got a pretty good bet going if I win, so help me out, okay? If I win, I get blow jobs for a week. Don't let me down! :)

Oliva: Dude. GROSS. I'm not sleeping with him just so you can get some BJs.

Vada: Sorry about that. He thinks he's FUNNY. Don't worry, I smacked him for you.

Olivia: LOL, thanks. If it gets you two off my ass, I'll tell you this. Apparently, he was the star in my dream last night, and I said his name in my sleep. And of course, Maverick heard me too! I'm still embarrassed, and he obviously thinks it's hilarious.

Vada: OMG...that's amazing. Totally getting written in.

Olivia: Great. I'm glad my humiliation is inspiring you so much.

Vada: You should find out if he's a good kisser. Ya know, for the book's sake.

Olivia: Oh, of course, FOR THE BOOK I'll just throw all my dignity out the window.

Vada: Perfect, thanks!! :)

Olivia: I hate you.

She sends me a dozen kissy faces and hearts, and I roll my eyes and smile just thinking about her. I miss her a lot and wish we had more time to catch up and actually reunite.

Once we cross into New Mexico, I occasionally look out the window at the tall weed grasses and rolling hills. It's so damn green outside, and the setting is picture perfect. The sun is high in the sky, and I check the time against our itinerary. We're actually ahead of schedule for now, probably because Maverick doesn't know how to drive the speed limit on these country roads, though I'm not complaining.

As I stare out the window, the thought of Maverick naked fills my mind, which only annoys me because I don't want to think about him like that. It doesn't help that I've had to smell the light hint of cologne on his skin all morning either. I swallow hard, trying to push the thoughts away, but it's no help. The sexy V led straight down to his cleanly shaved...

"Hey," he says, and I nearly jump out of my seat. He hasn't said a word for hours.

I place my hand over my chest.

"You're jumpy as hell," he says, chuckling. "Are we stopping in Raton? We're about twenty minutes away."

"Yes. We'll need to fill up, and there's a really good steak house I want to try." I don't think I can eat any more fast food, so I did a quick Google search yesterday. The place has rave reviews.

"Perfect. You know how I love my steak," he says, speeding up.

Soon we're crossing the overpass and heading into Raton. The town is small with most businesses on the main strip. We stop and get gas, then continue to the steak house.

"K Bobs?" He pulls into the parking lot and turns off the car.

"The reviewers said it was awesome. I swear," I tell him, half-tempted to pull it up on Yelp. Instead, I get out of the car, and he follows. We walk inside, and I'm happy to see the restaurant is full of people. We're seated instantly, and our order is taken soon after. The silence draws on between us, and I don't really know what to say, considering I moaned his name all night after seeing his anaconda dick.

"So…" he says before drinking half of the glass of water that was set in front of him. "What's your favorite color? Fave TV show? Or maybe for you, favorite book?"

"Are we playing fifty questions now?" I give him a look that says I'm less than amused.

"My favorite color is red. Mainly because it symbolizes power and can convey many different emotions. Love. Hate. Anger. Passion."

I swallow hard, watching him. He's trying, so I decide to play along.

"I like the color black because it matches everything."

He chuckles. "Even your dark soul."

Before I can get a word out, our food is placed in front of us. Maverick is still smiling at me as he cuts into his rare steak. "Even like my steaks to be red."

"You're gross. It's basically still mooing," I say, fully content with my chicken salad.

He puts a piece of the meat on his fork and reaches across the table. "Don't knock it till you try it."

"Thanks, but no thanks."

The waitress walks over and asks us if we need anything before placing our check on the table. I look at the time, thankful we don't have to rush.

"So what's on the schedule today?" Maverick asks before scooping mashed potatoes into his mouth.

I smile. "You really want to know?"

He nods and continues chewing. I give him a thorough rundown, actually impressed when he listens. Only took close to a week to make that happen.

After we're both finished eating, I pay the bill, and we

both stop to use the restroom before we go. I walk outside, and Maverick is waiting for me by the door. On the way to the car, I hold out my hand, and he gives me the keys. I'm starting to get used to this road trip stuff. Maybe one day I'll take one for pleasure. The thought of that makes me laugh.

We climb into the car, and I'm still smiling.

"What? Dreaming about me being naked again?" Maverick asks.

"No, that'd be a nightmare," I tell him as images of his abs and sexy V flash through my mind. *Ugh.*

"But you are now, aren't you?" His smug smile drives me nuts. I want to smack it right off his gorgeous, charming face.

I place the car in drive and try to ignore those thoughts. I glance at Maverick for a moment and see him watching me intently. Sometimes when he smiles, he has this small dimple in his cheek that's so damn cute. All I can do is shake my head as he sits there completely satisfied with himself for making me think about him naked all over again.

My mouth falls open as I try to soak in my surroundings as we drive out of Raton toward the mountains. The sky is so damn blue, and the grass is bright green. I follow the winding road until we're driving up in elevation through the pass and crossing the Colorful Colorado sign. Every once in a while, I catch a glimpse of the snowcapped Rockies.

We drive through Trinidad, and I'm mesmerized by the mountains in the distance.

"They're beautiful," I whisper.

Maverick turns and looks at me with a small smile. "That peak over there is Pikes Peak. There used to be a cog train you could take to the top, but I heard it's closed indefinitely. It's one of the coolest experiences I've had. Though Colorado is beautiful during the summer, nothing compares to this place in the winter when everything is covered in white. It's unbelievable and steals your breath away. Every Christmas growing up, my family would fly to Aspen for a ski trip. It became my second home."

I look at him then back at the road. "Wow. I wish I could see it snowed over. And how lucky were you for getting to spend Christmas in the mountains? You must be spoiled or something," I tease.

Maverick gives me a cheeky grin. "I have an older brother and a sister who's a few years younger, so there was no room for me to be spoiled. My parents just believed in us all being together and creating memories and family experiences during the holidays instead of giving us gifts we'd break or lose or grow out of. So each year, we'd take a big trip because we all loved the mountains so much. Looking back at it, those times are some of the ones I cherish the most, and I'm so grateful for them. What about you?"

"No siblings. I'm an only child. You're lucky. I always wished I had a brother or sister, and you've got both."

A hearty laugh releases from his lips. "There were times when I would've happily given them away. It's not easy being the middle child. I've had to prove myself all my life. Probably why I'm so good at modeling. Lots of practice fighting to be in the spotlight." He goes back to staring out the window.

The mood shifts in the car. There's something more, something he's not saying, so I try to change the subject.

"So you said you used to fly to Aspen? Do you just road trip there now?" I let out a laugh, but he doesn't react. He seems too lost in his thoughts.

"We don't travel for Christmas anymore. Haven't for a long time now," he vaguely replies.

I give him a smile then bring my attention back to the road. "Well, why not?"

Maverick runs his bottom lip between his teeth before speaking, and I don't dare rush him.

"It's okay. That was rude of me to ask. You don't have to answer," I say, not wanting to make him feel uncomfortable.

"No, no. It's fine." Maverick runs his hand along the scruff on his jawline, looking torn. While he's usually clean shaven, the past few days he's allowed the stubble to grow. He sucks in a deep breath and exhales it slowly. "When I was seventeen, my entire world tilted on its axis. Olivia, this isn't something that I typically talk about, so go easy on me, okay?"

I nod, not saying a word because I realize the seriousness of the situation just by his tone. The smile that once played on his lips is long gone.

"All my life, all I wanted to do was prove myself to my father. To show him I was trying to make my own mark in the world and that I was special too. My brother was the starting quarterback for his university, and my sister was a child genius. Then there was me, Maverick, and I had the middle kid syndrome. I realize that now. Anyway, after I started driving, I'd volunteer my time on the weekends at a local senior citizen home, and that's when I was "discovered" in a sense. A photographer caught a shot of me helping an older woman walk to a car, and it was placed on the front page of a bigger newspaper. I basically went viral. Modeling agencies contacted my parents because they ultimately had to give permission for me to work since I was under eighteen. I was booked solid after school and on the weekends.

My mother took it upon herself to be my agent, not allowing anyone to screw me over. Every penny I made, she put into a savings account for college. For the first time ever, I had my father's attention, and he was proud of me."

He glances over at me with sad eyes, and I give him a small smile of encouragement before he continues.

"My dad was a pilot and had been flying for nearly twenty years. He was doing private charter then, basically flying people back and forth like an air taxi. I had a meeting in New York with a big agency, and my dad was so adamant about flying me there, though he had clients he still needed to fly to Seattle. The plan was to fly from LA to Seattle, then take me to New York, but the plane was full, and there wasn't space for me to take the Seattle flight. I was so mad that I couldn't get on that plane. My mom booked our flights, paid a small fortune for them, and we flew commercial but ended up being delayed on our connecting flight due to weather. When we finally landed in New York, we got the call that my father was involved in an accident."

I swallow hard, and my mouth slightly falls open.

"He had clearance to fly to New York to meet us after he dropped his passengers in Seattle, and though the weather quickly shifted, he was certified to fly in those conditions. Due to mistakes he made, exhaustion, and other things, his plane went down." Maverick closes his eyes tight. "And I've blamed myself ever since."

Tucking my lips into my mouth, I try to get ahold of my emotions. I feel like such a bitch for saying anything about him refusing to fly. "I'm sorry. I'm so sorry."

I reach out and grab his hand and squeeze it. "And that's not your fault," I say, breaking our touch.

He lets out a stifled laugh. "Thank you. So needless to

say, I haven't flown since my plane touched down in New York. The anxiety I experience in airports is too overwhelming, and getting on a plane is something I don't think I could handle. So, if people want me to go on tours like these, they have to take me like I am, broken and completely fucked up, or I don't go."

I fully understand now. "It totally makes sense, and I don't blame you. And you're not fucked up or broken, okay? It's just more personal than most people realize. I get it. And I'm sorry for giving you shit earlier."

Finally, he smiles. "This is the reason I try to live each day like it's my last, Olivia. I shouldn't be here right now because I was supposed to be on that plane. And I don't know what divine intervention had me going another path, but there's a reason. A lot of people ask me why I continue to pursue this career so hard, and the truth is, I want to continue to make my dad proud. He told me he knew I'd go far, and I'll spend every day for the rest of my life proving him right."

"I think you already have," I tell him and mean it.

When he looks into my eyes, that's when I feel the shift. There are unspoken words streaming between us, and it's almost too much for me to handle.

Thankfully, the GPS interrupts the moment and tells me to take an exit toward downtown Denver. The tall buildings steal our attention as we search for our hotel. People are riding bicycles and scooters while others are happily running on the side of the road. I lower the windows and allow the fresh mountain air to swiftly blow through the car.

I continue driving down 16th Street, pass the Tattered Covers Bookstore where Rachel's signing is, then make a right toward the hotel. It's walking distance from the bookstore, and I internally do a small victory dance because it's a bit closer than I originally thought. After I pull into the valet lane, I unbuckle and look at Maverick.

"Remember to be on your best behavior," I playfully remind him.

"What happens in Denver, stays in Denver." He chuckles.

"So, about that video you took of me sleep talking..."

Maverick gives me his signature smirk. "There's no video. I was just fucking with you."

My mouth falls open. "Was I really sleep talking then?"

He conveniently doesn't answer. "Just by the look on your face, I already know I was the leading man in your sexy dreams last night."

I let out a loud groan, and we're right back to where we were this morning, me imagining him naked. "Sometimes you're a real asshole."

I step out of the car and Maverick grabs our bags from the back and follows me inside. Just as we've done at every other hotel we've stayed at during this trip, I check in with the front desk as he waits for me off to the side. After the paperwork is signed, I hand him his room key, and we go our separate ways. But this time, if he would've asked me for a drink or dinner, I might've reconsidered. Though I like spending my time alone, it's nice to have another person around, even if they only intend to annoy the shit out of me.

Maverick Kingston might not be the man I thought he was originally.

Mr. Playboy might actually prove *me* wrong.

CHAPTER TWELVE

MAVERICK

I'D BE LYING if I said I didn't miss Olivia when she's not around. It gets lonely in the hotel room all alone. I actually liked sharing a room with her, but I won't admit that to her. Not yet anyway.

However, I wasn't lying about her moaning my name in her sleep. The first time I heard it, I thought I'd imagined it. A few moments later, she said it again, and that time I knew for sure I wasn't hallucinating.

Though I enjoyed giving her shit about it, I could see how embarrassed she was. It gave me a thrill to know she'd been dreaming about me. She pretends to hate my guts all day, but her subconscious betrayed her, and now I know I'm slowly breaking her down. She may live her life on a strict schedule, but I can see something deeper is going on in that head of hers.

I never expected to open up about my dad to her like that, but something felt right at that moment to tell her. I don't share that part of my life with many people, in general, but she's actually easy to talk to when she's not scowling at or scolding me.

The next morning, I woke up early to hit the gym and then enjoyed watching the sunrise from my balcony. Olivia found us a great hotel right in downtown Denver, and the view is incredible. The air is crisp, and the sun's warmth promises a great day.

Just as I'm getting out of the shower, a loud pounding on my door echoes throughout the room.

"Maverick!" *Bang, bang, bang.* "Let me in!"

Rushing to the door, I tighten my towel around my waist and quickly open it up to a frazzled Olivia.

"Please tell me your room has an iron? Rachel's shirt got wrinkled, and she's freaking out. The iron in my room is about a hundred years old, and reception said it'd take about thirty minutes for them to bring me a new one."

"Uh…" I smirk as my eyes gaze down her body. "Sure. I mean, let's go check if it works." I step to the side to let her in.

"Thanks. I'm sorry to be intrusive, but when Rachel is having a freak-out moment, it causes *me* to freak out."

"I never would've guessed. You're handling this so well," I say dryly, holding back a laugh.

Her face falls as she gives me a deadpan look. "You have no idea what it's like to work for a woman like Rachel. She is sweet as pie to you and everyone else, but when things don't go her way, I'm a punching bag."

"Olivia." I place my hands on her nearly bare shoulders. "Relax, okay? You can handle this. Deep breaths."

She actually listens, and I watch as her chest rises and falls a few times. Her luscious tits on display are making it hard to be a gentleman and not stare.

"There. Perfect. Now I'll get the iron for you."

"Thank you. Assuming this is even the shirt she decides to wear." She huffs. "She's been extra difficult today."

I return with the iron in hand and perk a brow at her. "Today just started."

Olivia grabs it from me and sighs. "Exactly. Not enough goddamn coffee or liquor in the world for this."

She starts walking toward the door and right before she opens it, she glances at the closet door with the mirror on it. Then I watch her do a double take and do my best to refrain from laughing.

"Oh my God!" She immediately tries to cover herself up with her arms.

"Not the worst way to start my day." I cross my arms over my chest and flash her a smug smile.

"You could've said something! Just letting me walk around without a shirt on." She turns as if that's going to erase the image of her in a black lacy bra out of my head.

"I thought you were going for a new look," I tease. "Guess you weren't lying about black being your favorite color, though."

"Maverick. Shut up. I'm leaving now." I can see her reflection in the mirror, and she's squeezing her eyes tightly.

I walk up behind her and unwrap the towel from my waist. "Here, take my towel and walk back to your room." I drape it over her chest and around her neck to cover her up.

"Please tell me that's not the same towel you were just wearing." Her breathing picks up.

"Take a look for yourself," I say close to her ear with amusement.

A deep rumble echoes from her throat as she slowly peeks an eye open. She doesn't look in the mirror, though;

she keeps her head up as if she's purposely not focusing on it.

"As considerate as that is, I think I'd just rather go topless down the hall."

Her nervous tone makes me laugh.

Leaning in closer, my bottom lip brushes right on the edge of her ear. "Just take the towel. You shouldn't be showing your gorgeous tits off to just anyone anyway."

Her breath hitches, and when I place my hands on her shoulders, I feel her entire body tense. "Now go, so we aren't late," I say in a light, playful tone. She's always on my ass about time, so it's only fair to turn the tables every once in a while.

I lead her to the door, and she carefully opens it, making every effort to keep her gaze on the ceiling. "See you soon," I taunt before shutting the door.

"That wasn't funny, Maverick!" she shouts from the other side.

"Really? Maybe you need to work on that sense of humor of yours!" I'm totally messing with her, but it's too easy. Olivia Carpenter, the self-proclaimed perfectionist, is a hot mess.

I hear her groan before storming off.

Today's event is a signing in downtown Denver at Tattered Covers Bookstore. I remember Olivia pointing it out when we arrived. It's a cute local shop, and I'm kinda curious why she picked this store, considering Rachel's high-maintenance status.

Olivia: Rachel's making me find her a gluten-free pumpkin muffin before she'll go to the event, so you're gonna have to meet us at the bookstore

instead considering I'm going to have to walk a freaking MILE just to find one. She could have picked something easy like blueberry or chocolate, but NO! She thinks it's freaking pumpkin spice season or something! IT'S SUMMER!

I try not to smile at her outrage, but seriously, it's just too adorable. I can envision her voice as I read over her text, having a complete meltdown over this. The fact that she has to stress about the most ludicrous things makes me feel bad for her and a little guilty. I've given her so much shit for her obsessive need to be punctual that I haven't given much thought as to *why* she acts the way she does.

Given our bonding moment we shared yesterday, I'm curious to know more about her. What brought about her being an assistant? Where did she grow up? Why does she walk around like everyone she meets is going to hurt her or worse—leave her. She doesn't trust easily, that's a given, but there's more to her, and I want to know what it is.

Maverick: Deep breaths, Olivia! Why don't you let me help? I'm sure there must be a dozen cafes or bakeries around here.

Olivia: Yes, you would think! But pumpkin isn't as common apparently, and everyone keeps giving me weird looks as if I've lost my mind. Hell, maybe I have finally!

Sweet Jesus, this girl is going to pop a blood vessel if she doesn't calm down soon.

Maverick: I'm ready to go, so let me come and help you. Where are you right now?

Olivia: The corner of 16th and Wazee. Take a right out of the hotel.

Maverick: Okay, stay put. I'll be right there!

Grabbing my phone and wallet, I shove them both into my pockets and rush out of my room. Once I'm downstairs, I jog out the doors toward Olivia's location. Within a few minutes, I can see her pacing, pounding away on her phone.

"Hey," I say casually as I get closer.

"There's a place three blocks down that I haven't checked yet, and there's a bakery half a mile away." She finally looks up at me, and it nearly knocks the air out of my chest. Olivia has her hair all curled in loose waves, and it looks even blonder in the bright sunlight. Her plump lips are covered in a ruby red color, and I can smell the perfume lingering off her exposed collarbone. *Fuck me.* Olivia looks fucking gorgeous. "There's no way I can check both and get back to Rachel on time without her—"

"Olivia, I'm here to help, remember?" I step closer, demanding her attention. "I'll go to the bakery, and you go to the cafe. Text me if you find one, and I'll keep looking if neither have any."

She exhales a deep breath. "Okay, got it."

We part ways, and I shamelessly jog down the street until I see the sign for A Baker's Dozen and rush inside. The place is a sweets and carb addict's heaven, and if I weren't in a rush, I'd probably take a dozen for myself.

"May I help you?" a sweet, older woman asks.

"God, I hope so." I chuckle. "I'm hoping you have a pumpkin muffin? Gluten free."

"We do. We have twenty-six flavors available and—"

"Perfect, I'll take three please."

"Of course, sweetie."

As she bags my items, I quickly grab my phone and text Olivia.

Maverick: Maverick saves the day again! Meet you back at the hotel in five.

Olivia: OMG! I could kiss you right now! Thank you!

My eyes widen in surprise before another message comes through.

Olivia: But just for the record, I won't. So don't get any ideas, perv.

And there's the feisty, blunt Olivia I know.

Laughing, I shake my head and put my phone away so I can pay the lady.

"You got me a muffin?" Olivia asks as soon as she opens the bag. We're on the elevator to Rachel's room, and the smell is making my stomach growl.

"Uh, no. One for Rachel, two for me." I playfully pat my stomach.

Her face drops and she scowls at me. "Would it kill you to be pleasant, just once?"

I shrug, reaching into the bag and snagging a muffin. "It might." I flash her a quick smile before taking a large bite.

Once Rachel's muffin is delivered, I meet Olivia back down in the lobby so the three of us can walk together to the bookstore.

"Let me take that," I tell Olivia when I see she's carrying two large boxes. I don't wait for her to respond before taking them from her hands and holding them close to my chest.

"I was fine," she tries to argue, but I ignore it.

"Such a gentleman, Maverick," Rachel gloats.

"Always." I flash her a wink, and Olivia makes a show of rolling her eyes at me. "What? I am."

We're at the bookstore within ten minutes, and the aroma of old books hits my senses as soon as we walk in through the back. The front already had a line out the door of readers waiting to meet Rachel. It's a quaint little place, and as I follow Olivia's lead, I look around and see the endless rows of books and people walking around.

"You can put the boxes here." Olivia points to the floor next to a table. "I need to set out the little gift bags quickly," Olivia orders. I do as she says, but I take it upon myself to help unload them for her and put them in neat rows. There's a smaller table in the front with banners and signs of Rachel's picture and then another large banner with a picture of just me.

"Where did that come from?" I nod my head toward it.

She quickly looks over her shoulder to see what I'm referring to.

"Oh, you mean the Ian life-sized banner of you?" She chuckles. "The publisher sent it. Be prepared to take about a hundred pictures in front of it."

"Really? It's not even my best side."

Olivia throws a bag at my head, and hearing her laughter causes me to laugh.

Once the bags are all set out and organized to Olivia's liking, she starts instructing me on the plans. "Rachel will sit and sign, and you'll stand nearby to sign and take pictures."

"There's only one chair."

"Yep. Rachel will allow pictures at her seat, and to keep the line moving, they can stand and take a picture with you at the banner."

"Okay. So should I take my shirt off now or—" I grin.

"Don't even start," she says with a laugh. "I'm sure they wouldn't argue it, though." She quickly points a finger in my face. "But don't."

I snatch her finger in my palm and hold it. "Don't worry, I only reserve that for you now."

A deep blush surfaces on her cheeks, and our eyes lock, holding each other's gazes. She knows I'm teasing, but there's an undeniable spark between us that she refuses to acknowledge.

"Hilarious. We need to let them know we're ready now." Olivia steps back, our hands releasing in the process. I watch as she walks away, admiring how her tight skirt hugs her body. Olivia doesn't need to reveal a lot of skin or show off her best assets for me to know she's gorgeous, and it's not only skin deep. She definitely has more to her than she shows.

For the next few hours, Rachel woos fans with her big, bright smile and chats them all up as if she didn't just make her assistant go on a muffin search party. She plays the part well. I've only seen a glimpse of her demanding side through emails and calls, but to witness it firsthand is eye-opening.

Part of me wants to ask Olivia why she puts up with it, but I know better than to get involved. I'm sure it's just part of the job when you work with someone as well-known as

Rachel Meadows. She's single, has no children, and is more attached to her dog than any other human.

I play the part while Rachel signs books, taking pictures and smiling when readers ask if I'll repeat a quote from the book with a Southern accent. Safe to say, I botch it completely, but they seem to appreciate the effort regardless.

"Can I get a picture with you and Julia?" one of the last fans asks, and I nod my head even though I don't know who she's talking about. I remain in front of the banner, waiting. "Can you get her attention for me?" She's pointing to the other side of the table where Olivia is standing, handing out the goody bags.

"Wait, who?" I ask.

"That girl with the blond hair over there," she persists, pointing aggressively at Olivia. "She looks just how I envision Julia, and getting a picture with the two of you would be amazing!" She squeals, nearly bouncing on the tips of her toes.

She looks so damn excited I don't have the heart to let her down. "Uh, sure. Let me get her attention."

"Olivia!" I whisper-shout, but she doesn't hear me. I step around the table and grab her elbow, pulling her toward me.

"What the —"

Olivia trips as I pull her and ends up smack against my chest. She swallows tightly and looks up at me with wide eyes.

I clear my throat. "A fan wants us to take a picture together," I try to explain, nodding my head toward the eager woman.

"What? Why?" She takes a small step back to look around me.

"She said you remind her of Julia?"

Recognition resonates in her face. "The heroine," she answers. "So she wants us to take a picture together?"

"Yep."

She bites down on her lower lip and looks uneasy.

"If you don't want to, I can tell her—"

"No, no. It's fine. It's just a picture," she says casually, walking around me to greet Rachel's reader. I furrow my brows in confusion at her hesitation one second and her willingness the next.

"Oh my God, thank you so much!" The fan hands her phone off to someone and then stands between Olivia and me.

We wrap our hands around each other's waists and smile at the camera. The other person takes at least a half dozen pictures and then the fan turns around and hugs us both.

"You two are so perfect for Ian and Julia! Can I get a picture of just the two of you?"

"Uh, yeah, of course," Olivia answers before I can.

The woman is bursting with excitement as she backs up a tad and motions for us to get close. Having my hands on Olivia and our bodies close causes all kinds of feelings to surface. She wraps her arm around my waist, and when I wrap mine around her shoulders, I pull her flush to my side. She looks up at me in surprise, and I just smirk back.

"Gotta give the fans what they want," I tease, giving her a wink.

She bites down on her lip again and looks down, but I can tell she's blushing. Even though we shared a bed the other night, we hadn't physically been this close before, but I'm not complaining. Olivia's small compared to me and she smells so goddamn sweet, I want to bury my face in her neck and inhale for days.

"Okay, ready?" The woman brings her phone up and starts snapping pictures. "Oh my God, you two are so damn adorable!"

Olivia and I look at each other at the same time, and when I smile at her, she smiles back.

"Thank you again so much!" She squeezes us one more time before walking away with her friend.

"Looks like you might have a career in modeling after all," I tease, both of us still posing although no one is taking our photo.

"Nah, I doubt there'd be enough room for me with your ego taking up all the space."

"Oh, I forgot you're already a comedian."

"It's not a joke if it's true," she taunts with a devilish smile, breaking apart and walking away, leaving me to wonder if she felt that same spark as I did or if it's completely one-sided.

...only one way to find out.

CHAPTER THIRTEEN

OLIVIA

MAVERICK. Maverick. Yesssss.

My eyes shoot open, and I feel the embarrassment the second I hear a knock on the door.

This time I *was* fantasizing about him while sliding my fingers under my panties.

Ugh, God. What am I even thinking?

"Olivia!" Rachel's voice on the other side of the door has me rushing to answer it.

"Hey," I say as soon as I whip it open.

Without a word, she shoves Angel into my arms and drops a bag at my feet.

"She needs to be fed and then walked exactly twenty minutes later. She likes to be brushed after her walk and then she takes her morning nap. Her food and things are in her duffle. Then I need my laundry done and ironed."

I swallow, scrambling to hold Angel without purposely dropping her. "Of course," I tell her.

"I'd also like a spa appointment for a massage and facial with the bonus package."

"Right, I'm on it. I'll call right now."

"Great." She starts to walk away then stops herself. "Oh and Olivia?"

"Yes?"

"I hope you haven't forgotten the rules regarding Maverick. I know you're working closely together, but the last thing I need is a breakup or scandal to ruin my business partnerships."

"Trust me, you have nothing to worry about," I remind her.

She purses her lips, tilts her head down, then scans her eyes up and down my body. "Good to hear. Text me when my appointment is set."

As soon as she walks away, I grab the bag and take Angel inside. I look at myself in the mirror and realize what she was looking at. I wore my silky shorts and tank top pajama set to bed last night, and now she probably thinks I have Maverick stashed away in my room somewhere. Considering she gave us an odd look when we posed for pictures yesterday, I can't blame her for reiterating herself, but honestly, that was just to make a reader happy.

When Rachel informed me last night that she'd need me to do some administrative errands today, I wasn't aware that was code for work bitch, although I really shouldn't have expected anything less. There's a packed scheduled tomorrow with the signing, but today there weren't any events. I was hoping to relax a bit and catch up on my work, but I should've known better.

When I finally have a second to breathe, I check my phone and all of Rachel's social media sites and emails. I follow a variety of hashtags on Instagram, so I don't miss anything that Rachel's books are tagged in, and just as I'm scrolling through them, I'm stopped by a picture of Maverick and me from the bookstore signing. My eyes linger over Maverick as his arm wraps around my waist and he holds me close to his side. I scroll to the right for a second picture, which is almost the same, except it's a shot of Maverick looking at me instead of the camera. Then I look down at the caption.

The real-life Ian and Julia! SQUEE! They are adorbs, for real! I love them so hard! #ShouldBeARealCouple #HowCuteAreThey #IShipThem #SwoonyCouples #RelationshipGoals #CoupleGoals #BestLookingCoupleEver

My eyes widen as I read the hashtags, and then I click on the comments and start reading. There are dozens of them. The majority along the lines of *Ahhh OMG! I ship them so hard! If they aren't dating in real life, I'll never believe in love again! They are the perfect Ian & Julia!*

I make myself stop reading them after a few minutes because they're making my head spin. Maverick and I are so different. I never imagined we'd *look* like the perfect couple, but staring at our picture has me reconsidering. Julia has the same hair color as me, and she's described as petite, average height, with green eyes. I never realized it before now that I look like her.

I take a screenshot of the pictures before I close out of the app and get back to work. Angel needs to go out again, and if I don't finish Rachel's laundry, she'll have an aneurysm.

Four hours later, I finally complete everything on Rachel's list. I'm exhausted and hungry, and on top of it all, I haven't talked to Maverick all day and have this weird desire to know what he's up to. Today was *his* day off, so he probably worked out and then ravished all the local single ladies.

Rachel has dinner plans, so I put Angel back in her suite after taking her out again. This dog is higher maintenance than Rachel sometimes.

Once I'm back in my room, I lounge around for an hour, then I pace the small space between the door and the desk trying to decide if I should reach out to Maverick or not. I skipped lunch and am now starving for dinner. Should I ask if he wants to grab a bite with me? Or casually ask if he's eaten yet? Maybe just mention I'm going to go find something?

Ugh, why am I overthinking this? I'm an idiot.

I'll just go down to the bar and order something to eat from there and head in to get a good night's sleep. Lord knows I'll be up early tomorrow, running around like a chicken with my head cut off for Rachel again.

Deciding to go with that plan, I grab my things and take the elevator down to the lobby. The hotel bar is just off to the side, and it actually looks cozy with a fireplace in the middle and couches surrounding it. I find a stool and wait for a server.

Once I place my dinner and drink order, I settle in and look around. It's a nice hotel, and it's actually quite large and busy with people walking around. Just when I'm about to dig my phone out of my purse, I glance near the fireplace and do a double take when I notice Maverick sitting in one of the chairs.

What is he doing? I look around the bodies standing between us and...*is he reading a book?* What the hell?

Who reads a book in a bar?

Why the hell is Maverick reading a book?

I don't know why this amuses me so much, but I'm also impressed. Though I'm not going to let him know that. He could be using his time off to go drinking, clubbing, or worse —hooking up with single random locals.

Since I have to wait for my food anyway, I figure I might as well go say hello to him. I walk over and stand in front of him.

Maverick has one ankle propped on his knee, and he's leaning back slightly against a pillow, looking so relaxed, settled, and calm.

"You know you're blocking the only good light I had," he mutters without looking at me.

I hold back a laugh. "What are you doing?" I ask with my hands on my hips.

He finally looks up. "I *was* trying to read. Is that okay?"

"I'm just surprised." I shrug.

"That I'm reading a book?" He furrows his brows.

"That you *can* read," I tease, nudging his knee with mine.

"I'm not all muscles and good cheekbones, you know. I won the fifth-grade read-a-thon challenge and have a personalized blue ribbon to prove it," he replies with a smug attitude, and it causes me to chuckle.

"That's the most pathetic thing I've ever heard," I say, laughing. "So what are you reading?"

"Book three in the Mistborn series," he responds, flipping the book over and showing me the cover. "Always been a fan of the series and thought I'd do a reread."

I take the chair next to him and grab the thick paperback out of his hand. Turning it over, I skim over the synopsis and smile. "Sounds interesting. I'll have to add it to my TBR."

"Your what?" he asks when I hand the book back to him.

"My TBR," I repeat with a laugh. "My to-be-read list. It's about a mile long."

"Oh, didn't know there was such a thing."

"Are you kidding? They have a whole website dedicated to adding books to your TBR and reviewing them online. It's where an author's hopes and dreams go to die, but it's popular among readers."

"That sounds brutal," Maverick replies, chuckling.

"Yeah, it can be. I've had to check all of Rachel's early reviews for her before release because she refuses to go there herself. That way I can give her the sugary version and skip over the harsh shit."

"People really say that bad of things on there about her books?" He looks at me as if he can't comprehend anyone saying a rude thing about Rachel's stories.

"Oh my God! You wouldn't believe the reviews I've read over there. Not just for her books either. Reading is all subjective, and readers will experience the same book differently. There is no way to make them all happy, which sometimes means the hardcore fans will get really upset when a book in her series doesn't go the way they wanted. Rachel tells the story that needs to be told within her heart, and that doesn't always mean it's the way her readers expect."

"Wow...no wonder she doesn't go on there then."

"It's for the best. She's told me from the start that reviews are for readers—not for authors—so she understands that not all her readers will like every book she writes. She likes knowing what the early reviewers say, and then after that, she lets it go and moves on to writing the next. At that point, what's done is done, and it's not like she's going to go back and rewrite the book."

"Guess I could understand some of her hostility then," Maverick teases. "Wow, I had no idea there was so much involved in the publishing world. Kinda blows my mind."

"When I first started working in this field, I thought I was an expert in social media marketing and what it took to promote a book, but I had a rude awakening. It's so much more than just writing a book and trying to get the word out into the world. It's connecting with readers and bloggers and networking with other authors. It's finding a balance between life and work and managing deadlines. It's timing and luck and figuring out when to actually start promoting a book and when to post about it and *what* to post. Rachel gets emails weekly asking for interviews, Q&As, character interviews...you name it, she's done it. On top of all that, she plots a book for a week before she even starts writing it. She writes out their character profiles, outlines each chapter, lists all the secondary characters, prints out images of the setting, and sometimes makes Pinterest boards for inspiration. It's this whole week where she's taping pieces of paper all around her office, dozens of Post-it Notes everywhere, and she's muttering to herself for hours. By the time she actually sits down to write the first chapter, she can visually see the entire thing in her mind and just writes like crazy. It's actually a really neat process to watch—ya know when I'm not being yelled at for more coffee." I smile, chuckling. "It actually gives me a new appreciation for all she does to give her readers the best story she can. I know I complain about her a lot, but she's truly a genius in her craft."

"If I didn't know any better, I'd say you were a hardcore fangirl." Maverick's genuine smile has me smiling right back. He reaches over and tucks a piece of my hair behind my ear. My breath hitches as his fingers linger along my jawline before his hand drops back to his lap. "Don't worry, I won't tell anyone you kind of like your boss."

I snort, blushing. "Thanks. I'd like to keep that under wraps."

The bartender shouts at me that my food is ready, and it brings me out of my Maverick-induced haze. I wave a hand at him so he knows I heard him.

"Would you want to come eat with me? You probably ate already, but—"

"I'd love to," he interrupts. "Let's go."

He follows me to the bar and places his order with a beer. We drink and chat without skipping a beat. It's not forced or awkward. Maverick continues to surprise me during this trip, and I actually find myself enjoying his company tonight.

CHAPTER FOURTEEN

MAVERICK

THIS MORNING, I woke up early and had a cup of coffee at the hotel cafe downstairs. I sit smiling, thinking about last night. Olivia is something else. Not only is she beautiful, sassy, and smart, but she's sincere and funny too. Before this road trip, I never imagined myself settling down with anyone, but now I find myself falling for a woman who is my exact opposite. To say she's the whole package is an understatement. My heart knows, and while I'm trying to ignore it, eventually I won't be able to.

After I finish my cup of coffee, I get a bagel to go, then head upstairs and get dressed. Before I get a reminder text, I head out the door, not wanting to be late. I'm actually getting the hang of this signing thing. Of course, each venue is different, but the situations are the same.

Before the signing, we had an early lunch event with Rachel's readers. As I sat next to Rachel and listened to her answer the same questions she'd been asked a hundred times already, I found myself glancing at Olivia who was too busy to eat. If one weren't paying any attention, it'd be easy to gloss over her because she tries so hard to blend in with the background.

In this room, Olivia is the real MVP for running Rachel's life so flawlessly. What's disheartening is Rachel doesn't seem to appreciate anything Olivia does for her—only expects it all. Just because she's paying Olivia doesn't mean she has to continue to treat her like trash, regardless of her author social status. It's actually starting to irk me, but I know I'm walking on thin ice, so I find myself biting my tongue.

After the brunch, Olivia gives me a detailed rundown of what the rest of the day will be like. While I found it annoying in the beginning, it's actually helpful to know what to expect, though I still give her shit for it. She secretly likes it, though, whether she'll admit it or not.

When the main doors open, readers flood in. The line is so long, I don't see the tail of it, just the beginning. Picture after picture and the day seems to pass by in a blur. I've talked to so many people today that I don't remember many of the conversations.

Randomly, I catch sight of Olivia running around for Rachel, helping readers, and the smile on her face never fades. Occasionally, our eyes meet, and it causes my heart to lurch forward, which is confusing and exhilarating at the same time. While busting her ass, she moves around the room flawlessly, as if it's her own personal stage, following cues and giving rehearsed lines. Olivia deserves a fucking Emmy for her performance today.

Once the signing is officially over, a group of older women basically hold me hostage. They give me a rundown of the entire plot of Rachel's series and why they love Ian so much. I smile and nod and watch Olivia over their shoulders, hoping she'll save me, but she doesn't. While I enjoy chatting about Rachel's characters, I honestly have no clue what the hell they're referring to nine times out of ten, though I'm beginning to catch on now.

While I listen to them talk and try to make eye contact, I notice Rachel is reprimanding Olivia, who continues to act as if it doesn't bother her as she cleans off the table. Rachel eventually storms away, and Olivia rolls her eyes, which makes me chuckle. The ladies who I'm chatting with eventually ask for a photo and then offer to hook me up with their granddaughters. Laughter erupts from my core as I politely tell them no thanks.

"So are you in a serious relationship then?" one of them asks me. She's wearing a shirt that says, *COUGAR*. The ridiculousness of it actually makes me smile as the light reflects and shines off it. I've learned there are zero boundaries at these events. Zero. And if you have any, every single one of them will be demolished, then backed over a few times.

"Not at the moment," I say.

"But there's a special lady," the other adds with a cheeky grin. "I can tell. There's a sparkle in your eye."

I playfully shake my head.

"There's no reason to be shy about it. But just know, honey, if it doesn't work out, my Carley would be perfect for you." She leans in a gives me a hug. "Or maybe I would."

"Oh watch out!" I playfully tell her as she blows me kisses. Then, just like that, she takes a handful of my ass in her hand before they walk away. In any other industry, that'd be considered extremely inappropriate. At these events, though, I've learned it's just another friendly way to say goodbye. Luckily, I'm not easily offended, though I'm surprised Olivia didn't step in and shoo them away.

"Grandma knows best," I whisper under my breath as I walk toward Olivia who is obviously flustered and pissed. She's slamming bookmarks and bracelets around like they insulted her.

"Everything okay?" I grab a bucket of lip balms from the table and neatly place them in the box she's taking her aggression out on. "Okay then."

She stops in her tracks, and the look on her face is frightening as hell. "Do I *look* okay? Rachel is extremely pissed at me because she saw herself tagged on Facebook and there's red lipstick on her teeth. Apparently, it's *my* fault because I didn't tell her. Honestly, I didn't fucking notice because she rarely smiles that big."

I'm trying really hard to understand this because it's so childish. "There's not really anything that can be done about it now, though. Right? It's done. It's over with."

Olivia shakes her head. "I will never live this down. I even got the 'importance of paying attention to detail' speech. Detail is my middle name," she grits out.

I notice she's about to squeeze the life out of two heart-shaped stress balls that Rachel's series name is printed on. I take them from her hands and place them in the box, then turn to face her, placing my hands on her shoulders to force her to look into my eyes.

"You're so goddamn tense right now; you're going to snap in two. Deep breaths. Shake off the bullshit. Okay?" My voice is soft when I speak to her, trying to bring her down from a level ten of angry. Just as the words leave my mouth, Olivia's phone starts dinging.

Not wasting a second, she pulls it from her pocket, unlocks it, and groans. "Great."

I search her face. "Now what?"

Olivia turns her phone around and lets me read the message.

Rachel: I'd like a slice of chocolate cake, gluten-free, low carb, with a side of sugar-free sprinkles. Also, Angel needs to be taken out and fed. I'm going to rest my eyes before my meetup tonight. So be quiet when you come in.

Olivia turns around and looks at the table that's still full of shit. She's about to have a meltdown.

"How about I take care of that, and you finish up here?" I tell her. We're standing so damn close to each other I can smell the sweetness of her skin.

I didn't expect her to agree with me, because that's just not in her character. "I'm sure Rachel wouldn't apprec—"

I place my finger over her soft lips, and she immediately stops talking. "I'll handle her."

Green eyes bore into mine, and I smirk as Olivia swallows hard. Reluctantly, I remove my finger from her mouth. Her lips slightly part, and at that moment, before she can even mutter a word, I'm so tempted to kiss her.

"Okay," she whispers, then nods. "Please make sure it's gluten free, low carb, and sugar free. Just buy her chocolate-covered cardboard at this point and call it cake." Olivia finally smiles.

"With all this charm I have, she'll take whatever I give her and eat it with a grin."

Laughter erupts from her. "Don't flatter yourself. The woman can smell gluten from a mile away."

Olivia pulls her business credit card from her back pocket, along with Rachel's room key and hands them to me.

"When you walk into her room, all the lights are going to be out, and the curtains will be shut. Don't say a word. Put the cake on the desk with some plasticware and grab that little shit stain of a dog and bring it outside. Trust me when I say Rachel will pretend you're invisible. She might not even notice it's you. Get in and out as quick as you possibly can, please."

"I can handle this. Just trust me," I tell her, giving her a wink of confidence.

"I do. And that's the scary part." She smiles.

"Ouch. Nothing like a compliment wrapped with poison. I'll be back. If she adds anything to her ridiculous fuckin' list, text me." For a moment, we hold eye contact and unspoken words stream between us.

"Thank you," she finally says, breaking the tension by walking back toward the table to finish packing.

I laugh. "You owe me. Like really, really owe me."

"Add it to my tab." Olivia smirks over her shoulder, and she looks so goddamn cute. I take a mental snapshot and walk out of the ballroom with a shit-eating grin plastered on my face.

Pulling out my phone, I do a quick Google search and find a place close by who conveniently has what Rachel wants, stupid sugar-free sprinkles and all. It takes all of ten minutes for me to get the cake that smells like sweet cardboard and head up to Rachel's room.

I swipe the key card, and the room is exactly how Olivia described it. I pull my phone out to see, place the cake on the desk, and see Angel who's wagging her tail at me. Quietly, I find the leash and snap it on her collar. This little dog is the sweetest thing in the world. I really don't know what Olivia is talking about.

As soon as I step outside and set Angel on the grass, she instantly finds a spot to go. Once she's finished, I pick her up and walk back to the elevator. The doors slide open, and I step inside, followed by a group of women. When I turn around with Angel, they all burst out into aww's.

"Her bows are so adorable," one woman says, petting her. Angel's little nub of a tail is wagging back and forth.

The elevator seems to stop at every floor on the way up to Rachel's, and eventually, I'm the only person left. Two more floors. Damn. The elevator stops once more, and Olivia steps in, which causes the air around me to evaporate. As soon as Angel sees her, she starts growling and barking like a maniac. I burst out into laughter because I swear it's like I'm holding two different animals when Olivia is around.

"Angel, shh. I was just complimenting your manners," I say between laughs.

"Isn't she the worst animal in the world?" Olivia asks, glaring at the dog.

My chuckles echo off the walls as the doors slide open, and we step out.

"I'll take her back, just in case." Olivia holds her arms out, and Angel is ready to bite her fingers off.

"No, I'll keep her. We can go together. I'm sure you need your arms for all the work you need to do. Did you get the boxes to your room?" I follow behind Olivia as she leads the way to Rachel's room.

"Yeah. The bellman took them for me." There's slight relief in her voice, and I'm happy she's a lot calmer than she was thirty minutes ago.

Pulling the key card from my pocket, I swipe it, and Olivia opens the door. The room is still dark. I take the leash off Angel as Olivia walks to her bowl with the flashlight on her phone activated and pours food into it.

"Olivia?" Rachel says from the black abyss. Olivia looks at me, places her finger over her mouth, and turns the flashlight off.

"Yes?" she asks quietly.

Rachel lets out an overdramatic sigh and takes her time before speaking up. My eyes are rolling so hard in the back of my head, but I honestly wish I could see Olivia's face right now.

"What do you need, Rachel?" Olivia asks her, flatly.

"Have you noticed how Maverick looks at you like you're a delicate flower?" Rachel asks.

Now I'm happy as fuck the lights are off.

"I think you're imagining things. The cake is on the table. I'll see you in the morning," Olivia quickly says.

Rachel doesn't say another word, and I hear Olivia walking toward me swiftly and nearly runs into me. I grab her by the shoulders and stop her, and we make our way through the suite. The two of us can't get the hell out of there quick enough. We step into the hallway, and Olivia is shaking her head. Annoyance is written all over her face.

"See how delusional she is?" she asks, walking toward the elevator with her fists clenched.

I nod and let out a nervous laugh, but I can't help but wonder if Rachel is right.

She actually might be.

CHAPTER FIFTEEN

OLIVIA

I'M FORCING myself to walk in front of Maverick because I'm so damn embarrassed by what Rachel said. My cheeks are hot, and I'm flustered.

A delicate flower? I roll my eyes thinking about it. For someone who's so eloquent with words, she could've used a better descriptor. Me and delicate don't go together, and I take pride in having my shit together, regardless if I'm forcing it half the time. Not to mention, Maverick doesn't look at me any differently from the way he looks at Rachel's readers. I would know; I caught myself watching him a little too often today. He's an absolute natural around people, giving them the attention they desire from him. There wasn't one woman who left his presence feeling less than. So she's just looking into it too deeply, searching for shit that's not there.

I step inside the elevator and hold the door for Maverick. He joins me, and I press our floor since his room is actually somewhat close to mine. An awkward tension lingers between us, and I'm not really sure what to say or if I need to talk at all, but the silence draws on, and it's almost too much for me to handle.

"I'm sorry you heard her be like that. I'm sure if she knew you were there, she wouldn't have said that," I tell him. His hazel eyes meet mine, and my heart lurches forward, beating wildly, and I try to push it down. Maverick gives me a half grin which practically makes me melt before the elevator doors open.

"If it makes you feel any better, I don't think you're a delicate flower, Olivia. You're strong and fierce. You're a badass."

My breath hitches, and I'm so damn happy I'm walking in front of him again so he can't see the blush on my cheeks. That might be the sweetest thing anyone has said to me. "Thank you."

"What are your plans tonight?" he asks me as I stop at my room, then laughs because he already knows. "Right."

I'm doing what I do every night—working. "You can join me if you want. Not sure I'll be the best company, but..."

"Let me go back to my room and grab some things, and I'll be back."

My eyes meet his. "I really have a lot of work to do."

With hands held up, he grins. "I promise not to be a bother."

His tongue slides out and licks his bottom lip, and I find myself staring. The man is sexy as hell without even trying. "Okay. Good."

As Maverick walks down the hallway toward his room, I enter mine, shut the door, and lean against it. My heart is beating so hard in my chest. I understand why women go crazy for him, but he's more than his looks. At that moment, I find myself smiling thinking about him, but then Rachel's voice subconsciously screams at me. Shaking my head, I push it all away. First of all, there's no way a man like him would ever be with someone like me. We're complete opposites. I really don't know why she's so damn concerned about it.

I grab my phone and see I have a message from Vada, more than likely looking for an update. Too bad she'll be sadly disappointed.

Vada: Did you find out his girth yet?

Olivia: Like a Coke can.

Vada: REALLY?!

Olivia: No, you perv!

Vada: Bummer. So what? Like an uncooked hot dog then?

Olivia: Omg. I have no idea.

Vada: So you're saying you haven't slept with him yet? How's that possible?

Olivia: Willpower, self-control, the desire to keep my job.

Vada: Boring, boring, and double boring. Why are you keeping yourself from that delicious hunk of man meat? I already told Ethan he's my hall pass.

Olivia: I don't remember you being this weird. Was I just clueless back then or oblivious to your quirks?

Vada: Both, I'm sure. I'm sleep deprived, and my nipples feel like hardened pepperoni. Give your girl something over here!

I snort at her choice of words. Between breastfeeding, pumping, and diaper changes, I imagine Vada is completely unhinged.

Olivia: We've been getting along, and I'm enjoying his company.

Vada: Okay, Grandma.

Olivia: What? That's the truth! We've had some "moments" I guess you could say, but we both know the rules. Plus, I don't just sleep around. Even if he was attracted to me that way, nothing could come of it. We live worlds apart, and we're complete opposites. It'd just hurt in the end when reality hit.

Vada: Liv. You know I love you, but you, my friend, are using avoidance techniques to keep your distance. You come up with any excuse as to why you shouldn't instead of following your heart and listening to the list of reasons why you should. You figure if you never go for it, you can't get hurt. You're trying to control everything in your life when, in reality, you just can't.

Olivia: But they aren't excuses if they're the truth, right? Say I sleep with him and I get even more attached and then at the end of the trip, we go our separate ways because that's what's going to happen. I live in Chicago, and he's in LA. What's the point?

Vada: Do you think when you're old and on your deathbed, you'll be thinking of all the things you did and regret them, or will you be thinking of all the things you didn't do and regret not going for it? That's what you have to ask yourself.

I hate that Vada can outsmart me in two seconds flat. She's an old soul, and although I hate that she's right—she's right. Will I walk away thinking what if, or will I walk away heartbroken? Or both?

Once I get a grip, I kick off my heels and change into sweatpants and a T-shirt, then grab my laptop and place it on the bed. A knock sounds out on the door, and I rush to open it. Maverick steps in, looks me up and down, and gives me a nod.

"Hi, have we met before?"

"Stop saying that," I tell him with a playful eye roll.

A laugh escapes his throat, and it sounds like music. That stupid smile fills my face again. Is it possible that Rachel is right? Do I look at him a certain way too?

Maverick walks inside with his book from last night and has a small laptop with him. I plop down on the bed, and he sits on the other side. Looking over at him, he shrugs at me, then kicks off his shoes.

"Well, just get comfortable," I tease.

"You set the precedence here, not me."

Shaking my head, I unlock my computer and log in to my email and task manager.

Rachel's publisher sent an email reminding her of all the confirmed deadlines. I get up and grab my planners and notebooks and set them beside me. Glancing over, I catch Maverick watching me.

"I know it's serious when you grab your author Bible. So I had an idea. How about we ditch all this nonsense and go out on the town."

With wide eyes, I stare at him. "Are you serious?"

"As a heart attack. All this bullshit will still be here tomorrow. Get dressed, and let's go have some fun."

I look at him like he's lost his mind. "Not happening."

"It's Colorado. We should take full advantage and grab some special brownies. After we're good and relaxed, we can hit up 16th Street," he says with a smile. "Nothing like weed and pizza."

"Are you sure you haven't already had some special brownies? Now shhh. I have to concentrate."

The room grows silent, but only for a short time. "So if I wanted to hire you as my assistant, what would I need to do?"

I glare at him. "I only take on one client at a time. And you can barely handle me now, so I doubt you'd want me running your life."

"Perfect. So fire Rachel and come work for me. All these flagged emails need replies. It's people who want to book me for a shoot." He turns his laptop around, and his email inbox is a freaking nightmare. Pages of people need a response, and my mouth drops open in shock. I'm horrified by all the flags, and how there's zero organization.

"Maverick. Holy shit. I have no words."

He shrugs. "That's a first. So next time you're talking about something I don't care to hear, I'll just flash my inbox, and that'll show you."

When our eyes meet, he smiles, and I watch as his gaze moves down to my mouth. Quickly, I turn my head and go back to my laptop. I'm imagining things, and it doesn't help that Rachel's words are on repeat in my head about how Maverick looks at me.

"Are you hungry?" he asks. "You're bound to be."

"I could eat." Today was busy as hell, and I've only had a nasty protein bar that I packed for Rachel that tasted like prunes. I get so caught up in work that I often forget to eat. It's nice to have someone remind me while everything is still open.

Maverick begins typing away on his computer. "Done. Food is on the way."

"What did you order?" I ask.

He laughs. "Something that's got all the gluten, carbs, and sugar."

"Thank God." I smile.

The room grows silent again, and soon there's a knock on the door. Maverick gets up and answers it, and as soon as I smell the food, my mouth begins to water. The door clicks closed, and he comes into view holding a large pizza box with plates stacked on top.

"Little did he know, two people are eating this whooooole thing." He places it on the desk and opens the top. The aroma of the cheese and bread causes my mouth to water.

"Get ready to eat the best mountain pie ever. And you have to try honey on the crust."

I grab a plate and stack a few pieces. "Honey?"

"It's the best shit in the world. I dream about this pizza." He takes a huge bite and lets out a moan.

I take a bite of pizza and do the same. "Oh my God," I say while chewing.

"Right, told you. Beau Jo's will change your life." He finishes a piece and slaps another on his plate. It amazes me how he can make pizza look sexy.

We eat until we're ridiculously full, and I'm pretty sure this is what a carb coma feels like.

I try to get back to work, but it's impossible. Once I start yawning, Maverick takes notice. My eyes are heavy, and I think it's from all the activities from today. Signings exhaust me.

"You need rest," he says, closing my laptop and moving it out of the way. I slide under the covers, and Maverick stands to pack his things. My eyes feel like bricks, and I'm so comfortable that I feel myself drifting off. I hear his laughter when my eyes finally close.

"Good night, my delicate little flower," he says with a small laugh as the lamp next to the bed clicks off. "See you before the sun rises."

"Night," I whisper before I slip away to dreamland.

With a racing heart, I sit up in bed and glance around,

making sure I'm alone. In my dream, Maverick was naked, walking toward me, and I was happily undressing for him. If I wouldn't have woken up, I know exactly where it would've led—the same place it's been going every night when he visits my dreams—his mouth on mine, my hands all over his body. Just thinking about it causes heat to rush through me, but I try to ignore it.

Unlocking my phone, I see I still have an hour before I'm supposed to be up, so I try to close my eyes and get more sleep, but it doesn't happen, which only frustrates me. I force myself into the shower to try to push the fantasies of him away. Though he doesn't make it easy for me when he wears clothes that hug him in all the right places. I let out a groan as I turn on the water and undress.

I try to busy my mind with the upcoming thirteen-hour drive and the signing in Vegas this weekend—anything that will lead me away from thoughts of Maverick—but somehow my mind keeps going back to him. Considering he appears in my dreams and my thoughts just makes me realize that I need to keep him at a distance. It's easy to pretend something's between us, but it's not reality. There are many reasons it would never work, regardless if my heart lurches forward each time I see him. I refuse to be another slash on his bedpost. Not to mention I need my job, and if Rachel suspects anything is going on between us, she'll fire me on the spot, and it's just not worth it. There's a line of people who'd die to be her assistant even though it's not full of glitz and glamour like they think.

After I'm dressed, I decide to read for a bit since I have time but realize I can't concentrate. Instead, I pull up my inbox only to find several emails Rachel's sent to her publisher about a summer tour she expects next year. Two weeks of my life on the road isn't so bad, but two months is pushing the line. I'm not sure I'd survive it. In reply after reply, Rachel has volunteered me to plan the entire thing and write up a proposal with the cost to be submitted by the end of the month. When I realize I'm grinding my teeth, I stand and try to shake off my annoyance, but it doesn't help. Thankfully, she gave me a year to plan it instead of three months, but damn, this might take a freaking village.

When my alarm rings out, causing me to jump, I realize I forgot to turn it off. I text Maverick and let him know when we'll be leaving, and I get a thumbs-up emoji in response. It's early, and I'm already in a shitastic mood. After I pack my stuff, I linger for another twenty minutes before I go to the lobby and wait for him. Surprisingly, he's right on time, which is impressive. Maybe I'm finally wearing on him.

I stand and wheel my suitcase outside.

"Well good morning to you too," he says, taking the keys from the valet.

After my suitcases are placed in the back, I get in the passenger seat. "Morning."

I flip open my planner for next year and try to nail down a practical schedule for a summer tour that doesn't interfere with any events Rachel already has planned. I'm so fucking frustrated and let out a huff.

"Everything okay?" Maverick turns down the music.

I glance over at him, then look back at my planner. "No."

"Want to talk about it?" He slows down at a stoplight, looks over at me, then yells, "Goat rodeo!" I'm so damn confused when he reaches for the handle, jumps out, and pretends he's riding a bucking bull as he runs around the car before climbing back into the driver's side. I burst out into laughter.

"Have you lost your mind?" I say between laughs as he gets back inside.

The light turns green, and he accelerates, then stops at another red light. Glancing over at me with the cutest smirk on his face, Maverick yells goat rodeo again. He does the same thing and gets back in the driver's side before the light turns green.

I'm laughing so hard, tears roll down my cheeks, and I can barely catch my breath. I glance over at a man in the car next to us, and he's shaking his head. Maverick waves at him with a grin.

"Better now?" he asks as he speeds up onto I-70. All I can do is smile and nod.

Soon the city is behind us, and I try to soak in the surroundings while I can, though I've heard the drive through this side of Colorado and through Utah is beautiful. The mountains disappear for a while, but then I see the top of the snowcapped mountains, and I can't keep my eyes off them.

"We should come back. You need to see Garden of the Gods. It's a must," he says as we drive through Grand Junction.

"Maverick." I look over at him. "You know good and well that after this trip we'll go our separate ways and never talk again unless it's about business."

His face slightly contorts. "Wow, that hurts. I thought we were getting friendship bracelets and all."

I snort, giving him a look. "We're two people who were forced to road trip together. I just don't want either of us to be confused about where we stand. You'll go back to California, and I'll go back to Chicago, and our lives will go on.

Don't get me wrong, it's been fun, but this is all it is. That's the reality."

The car grows silent and stays that way until we're in Utah. I almost feel bad, but it's the truth, and sometimes the truth hurts. Once we're at the halfway point, Maverick pulls over, and we have lunch. Just as I'm about to take a bite of my chicken quesadilla, my phone starts ringing. *Mother* flashes across the screen. I reject the call and Maverick notices but doesn't say anything.

We pay, get gas, and I check the GPS before I put the car in drive and head toward Vegas. My phone vibrates again. I glance at it, then reject the call. I cannot talk to her right now.

"Why aren't you answering your mom's call?" he finally asks.

I swallow hard, not really wanting to discuss it, and stare out at the mountains. Maverick shared so much with me about his dad that I feel guilty about wanting to keep that part of my life from him. Sometimes it's better not to talk about my past because then it's almost as if it never happened. When I don't answer his question, he stares out the window, and I feel an invisible wall being built. Considering this trip is almost over, and we won't be hanging out again, I suck it up.

"It's because she probably wants money or something. I don't have the best relationship with my mother, and my father is nonexistent. My family life isn't the greatest. It's actually kinda fucked up."

He doesn't look at me with pity or sadness, and relief floods through me. "I don't know anyone who has a perfect family life. Everyone has skeletons."

I give him a small smile. "She's the reason I'm the way I

am. It's important for me to have control of my life because for so long I didn't. It's why I live and die by my schedule. My father left us when I was a baby, and I don't actually remember him at all, and my mom struggled to keep a job for years. She's the type of woman who needs to be wanted by someone, and growing up, I witnessed that. My father leaving us ultimately destroyed her."

Maverick doesn't say anything; he sits there and listens.

"Eventually, she met the wrong man who introduced her to drugs, and it helped her push away the pain. At thirteen years old, I watched her destroy her life, one hit at a time. While love and that feeling of being wanted once ruled her, it was replaced with shooting up. When I was sixteen, she met someone who really cared about her. He was a stand-up guy and tried to get her help, but she refused. She chose drugs over him, and eventually, he left us too. This only caused her to enter another downward spiral. There were weeks when I didn't see her, didn't know where she was, but I kept it all inside while trying to finish high school."

"Wow, Olivia. I'm sorry," he offers, shaking his head.

"A week before I graduated high school, I came home and found her face down on the floor. I called 911 and did CPR until the ambulance arrived. That day, I thought she was going to die, and I'd be put into foster care until my eighteenth birthday. I was so scared and sad, because she was all I had, but I was never enough—I wasn't enough for her to stay clean. She needed companionship so much that she was willing to die for that. My entire life was chaos until I left home for college. So no, I don't always answer her calls because she usually wants something from me—which is the only time she ever reaches out—and I don't have time to deal with that right now. I have my own problems." My words come out harsher than I intended.

"I understand. I really do. Do you know where your dad is now?" he asks.

"Living in New York. He offered to take me in when shit got really bad, but I couldn't leave my mother. We have an okay relationship, but he was barely there for me. And any money he sent, my mother spent on drugs. I learned at a young age to take care of myself," I tell him.

"My opinion still stands. You're an absolute badass. I have so much fucking respect for you." His words are sweet and sincere, which I appreciate more than he'll ever know.

My phone vibrates again, and this time, Maverick rejects the call for me. The rest of the way we talk about things that aren't so personal—music, TV shows, Netflix series binges, and the beaches in California. Soon we're making our way into Las Vegas, and when I pull up to a stoplight, I look over at him and smirk.

"Goat rodeo!" I yell out and reach for my door handle. Maverick steps out and starts his bucking bronco movements, and I shut my door and accelerate. In the rearview mirror, I watch as he lifts his arms up in the air. I'm laughing so hard as he walks a block toward me. He opens the door and sits inside, and I'm huddled over, laughing my ass off.

"I owe you one for that! The woman at the light was so confused. She hurried and locked her door like I was going to rob her," he explains with a smirk.

"I know. I watched her mouth fall open when I drove off," I try to explain through my laughter.

"Just wait, I feel so sorry for you. I don't get back, Olivia. I get *even*," he playfully threatens.

I sarcastically nod. "Suuuure."

By the time we make it to our hotel, my face hurts from laughing so much. We get out, and I check in. I hand him his key, and he pretends to be mad.

"I'm going to get you when you least expect it," he warns as he walks toward the elevator.

I follow him. "Good. I look forward to it."

CHAPTER SIXTEEN

MAVERICK

I LOVE WATCHING Olivia finally loosen up and laugh until her face turns red. She's gorgeous without even trying, but when she stops overthinking everything and just relaxes, she's stunning. Simply beautiful.

"So what are you going to do on your first night in Vegas?" I ask her when we reach our floor.

"I'm exhausted, so I plan to order room service, take a hot bath, and go to bed." She drags her roller suitcase behind her, and I can't help but watch the sway of her hips rock back and forth. She stops at her room and turns to look at me. "What are you gonna do?"

"I have a couple of friends here actually and told them I'd hit them up once I arrived. Other than that, I'm not sure. Probably hit the Strip."

She bites down on her lip and lowers her head, scanning her eyes over my body. Even when she's trying to be subtle about it, I catch her every time.

"Well don't forget we have a very packed schedule

tomorrow," she finally says, scanning her key card. "Rachel will—"

"I know, Olivia." I step forward, pinning her with my eyes. "I won't be late." I toss her a wink before walking to my room a few doors down. Just before I step inside, I lean back and see she's still standing in the hallway. "Good night, Olivia."

"Uh yeah, night. See you tomorrow." She scrambles to get inside as fast as she can with her luggage.

Waking up in Vegas is a complete experience all on its own. The sun is bright as fuck, the streets are filled with cars and people walking around, and it's as if no one even went to sleep. Everyone is still on the go, ready to keep the Vegas atmosphere alive.

According to Olivia's schedule, Rachel has a bookstore signing off the Strip and then a luncheon meet and greet with seventy-five VIP readers. After that, Rachel is meeting with some locals to gamble, which means Olivia and I will be on our own after dinner.

"Good morning," I say as soon as Olivia opens her door. I push off the wall and hand her a Starbucks cup of her favorite drink.

"Mornin'..." she replies slowly, narrowing her eyes at me

suspiciously. "You're looking bright-eyed and bushy-tailed for this early."

"Don't I always?" I feign offense. She ignores me and sips her coffee as if it's her lifeline.

"You ready for today?" she asks as we make our way into the elevator.

"Ready as I'll ever be."

Olivia presses the button for the third floor where Rachel's private signing is being held. This event is different from the others because it's not in a bookstore or in a large ballroom with dozens of other authors. From what Olivia's told me, Rachel will participate in a Q&A, and then the readers will have the opportunity to get their books signed.

"You'll be sitting up there with Rachel, but the majority of the questions will be for her," she informs me.

"And you'll be doing what?"

"I'll be the emcee, asking the questions. After polling her reader group and Facebook page, I spent three months researching and narrowed the list of most frequently asked questions down to thirty. Her readers should enjoy it. Then if there's time afterward, I'll let the audience ask a couple of questions too."

"Wow...pretty intensive process," I half-joke with her, but honestly, I'm not even surprised anymore. Olivia doesn't do anything half-assed, and that's part of the reason I respect her so much.

I follow Olivia into the back way through a private room and am surprised to see Rachel is already there, talking to one of the hotel workers. There's a small stage up front with a table and chairs and a podium with a microphone. She's rambling off orders, demanding a beverage station, more chairs, and less of a "breeze," whatever that means.

"Olivia, about time." Rachel finally turns and acknowledges her. "Angel needs to be let out in about twenty minutes. I'd like a plain bagel with fat-free cream cheese, *not* toasted, and I've decided to have Maverick emcee the Q&A, so you'll need to give him the list of questions."

My head shakes to make sure I heard Rachel correctly. Looking at Olivia, she stands frozen in place, nodding as she listens to all her orders. I can't believe she's just taking it and not even arguing with her, considering Olivia just told me how much work it took to get this together. I wouldn't feel right taking her place, not to mention I wasn't even asked properly.

"I'm not sure that's a good idea," I finally blurt out, unable to hold back after seeing Olivia's face drop. "Olivia is more prepared. She knows the books. I-I'm just the image."

"Oh, that's why it'd be perfect!" Rachel singsongs, walking toward me with a bright smile. "They'll be glued to you and really take a lot from the whole experience."

I look over Rachel's shoulder and see Olivia's face. She gives me a tight head shake to tell me not to argue with her, though I'm really tempted. This is a shitty thing for her to pull at the last second.

I nod, giving Rachel my approval, and when I do, she squeals and nearly blows out my eardrums. After that's settled, Olivia and Rachel talk about the volunteers out front who are taking the readers' tickets and making final touches.

Four hours later, my throat is dry and raw after hosting the Q&A and then chatting with readers during the signing. As far as I know, everything went great, and Rachel and her readers left happy.

"Well, if your modeling career doesn't take off, at least you know you have a knack for hosting," Olivia says as we make our way back to our rooms. "Could be one of those TV game show hosts where they wear fancy suits and drink twenty-dollar bottled water." She forces out a laugh, but I see right through it.

"Olivia, stop." She turns but doesn't look at me. I bring a finger under her chin and tilt her head until our eyes meet. "Why did you let her walk all over you like that? I hated taking that from you."

She shrugs, and I reluctantly drop my hand. "Because it's my job to make her happy. It doesn't matter what I want or what I do on the side. Rachel always gets what she wants, and it's just easier to let her do things her way when she changes her mind."

"Just because it's easier doesn't mean it's right."

"Not in my world," she states. "What's it matter anyway? The readers were happy to listen to you talk and crack jokes, so that's all that really matters in the end."

"I wish Rachel knew everything you go through to please her. She takes you for granted. That's easy to see," I tell her sincerely. "We should go out tonight. You need a drink or ten." I flash her a smile, hoping she'll give in.

"I don't know. Rachel has that author reading tomorrow afternoon and..."

"Stop making excuses, Olivia. C'mon. Just one drink." I pout out my lower lip and make pathetic whimpering noises. "Don't make me get on my knees and beg because I will."

She snort-laughs and pushes against my chest. "You're full of shit."

Without missing a beat, I fall to my knees and put my hands out in a pleading hold, batting my eyes with the biggest frowny face I can muster. "Olivia, *please!*" I shout loudly, knowing she'll cave once I start embarrassing her. "Please! Please, please, please!"

"Oh my God!" Olivia squeals, pulling at my hands to lift me, but she's a weakling compared to me. "You're insane! Get up!" She's laughing now, and I know I have her on board. "Fine! Okay, let's go, you psycho!"

"Yes! Victory is mine!" I throw my fist into the air and celebrate.

"One drink! Got it?" she warns me with her puny little finger in my face.

Approximately six mixers and three shots of vodka later, Olivia and I are feeling every ounce of liquor. I'm not sure how many I've had or how many she's had, but the table between us is filled with empty glasses.

"Oh my God, I have an amazing idea!" Olivia shouts over the music, but she's close enough that I can hear her without her shouting. "We should find a karaoke bar!"

"A karaoke bar?" I question. "Are you finally going to serenade me?" I tease. I'm definitely not drunk enough to do karaoke, but Miss Lightweight passed tipsy and buzzed three drinks ago.

"We should do a duet! Oh my God, yes! Let's go!" Olivia bounces in her seat and is on her feet before I can comprehend exactly what she just said. I'm living for this version of her, knowing it's a side I'll probably never see again.

It takes us all of five minutes to find a karaoke bar, and as soon as we walk in, Olivia drags me to the DJ booth to sign us up. I have no idea what she told the guy, but it doesn't matter because he hands us two microphones and then Olivia pulls me up on the mini stage.

"Are you ready?" she asks with the biggest smile.

"That depends. What'd you pick?" I ask her, but as soon as the music starts, I immediately know. "Ah, good choice!"

"It's a classic! I love this song!"

Sonny & Cher's "I Got You Babe" plays loudly over the speakers as the lyrics flash across the little screen in front of us. We sing our parts and then come together for an off-key duet, but it doesn't matter because singing up here with Olivia is the best time I've had in a while. She's laughing and smiling, and even though her pitch is awful, at the same time, it's all perfect. She's not fidgeting with schedules or worrying about controlling anything, and I've never seen her so loose and happy.

We sing the last line, and I take her hand so we can give our audience of fewer than five people a proper bow. They clap with little amusement, and after we hand our microphones back to the DJ, I keep her hand in mine and drag her to a bar top table.

"You are amazing," I tell her sincerely, grabbing a piece of hair stuck to her cheek and tucking it behind her ear. "You were having the time of your life up there."

"I know." She laughs. "You're a good singing partner."

"I told you, I'm a man of many talents." I wink, but her eyes are locked on my mouth.

I swipe my tongue between my lips and watch as her chest rapidly rises and falls. She bites down on her bottom lip, and I bring my finger up to pluck it from her teeth.

"Olivia."

She blinks and brings her eyes to mine. We share a silent moment, but no words are needed to know what we're both thinking. I lean in and dip my head down and carefully brush my mouth against hers, swiping my tongue gently between her lips as I seek entrance. She doesn't pull back, so I take that as a good sign to continue. I wrap a hand around her neck and pull her body into my chest as I cover her mouth with mine. Olivia fists her hands in my shirt and slides her tongue against mine, and soon we're devouring each other, both begging for more.

The moment is getting heated, too heated for a public location, so I unwillingly pull back slightly. "Olivia…" I say between heavy panting. "We should go back to the hotel before—"

"I can't wait that long," she nearly purrs. "I want you right now."

This is definitely not the Olivia I've grown to know the last week and a half, and the last thing I want to do is take advantage of the fact that she's drunk.

"Olivia, we don't have to. You've been drinking and—"

"Maverick, I'm throwing myself at you, and you're going to tell me no?" She pulls back, giving me a look of shock and hurt. "I'm a big girl and can prove to you I'm just fine to make big girl decisions. Want me to walk a straight line and touch my nose? Or say the alphabet backward? ZYXWVUT…"

"Olivia, stop," I say, laughing at the fact that she would have the alphabet memorized backward. "Okay, I believe you."

"Good, now kiss me." She wraps both hands around my neck and pulls our mouths back together.

Fuck, she tastes so damn good. I want to lift her onto this table, push her legs apart, and slide inside her so goddamn deep she'll be feeling me long after this trip ends.

"Let's at least go somewhere private," I plead with her, grabbing her hand and leading her out of the middle of the bar. I have a feeling Olivia has never had sex outside of a bed before, and this wild side of hers is dying for something new. I find a hallway that leads to the restrooms and probably a storage room or two, but before dragging her down there, I turn around and make her face me. "Do you trust me?"

"I trust you not to murder me if that's what you're asking."

I laugh and pull her lips back to mine. "You're adorable. Good enough for me."

Luckily, we ended at a bar off the Strip, and it's not crowded, so I take her into the ladies' bathroom, figuring it'd be the cleaner of the two. As soon as we step inside, I pull her up until her legs are wrapped around my waist, and her back is pressed against the door. She squeals with laughter as I lock the door.

With Olivia's arms wrapped around me and mine holding her ass up, we devour and taste one another. I'm so fucking hard, I know she can feel it against my jeans. I press against her, and when she moans, it's like an electric current has a direct line to my dick.

"Olivia, tell me you want this," I demand. "I need to know you won't regret this in the morning."

"I want you, Maverick. But that doesn't mean I won't regret it. All that matters is I want you right fucking now."

I pull back slightly and set her down on her feet. "That's not good enough. Get out of that head of yours and tell me you won't hate me for this later."

"I promise, I won't hate you. But I really want you to fuck me, so if you don't, then I'll definitely hate you."

Laughing, I wrap one hand around my neck and pull my shirt over my head. "Fuck, you're even hotter when you're a demanding little vixen."

Scooping her up, I carry her to the counter that's actually

semi-decent and start undoing her pants. She never changed out of her work clothes, so she's in one of those pantsuits.

"Is it weird I'm now oddly attracted to these business suit things you're always wearing?" I tease.

"Oh yeah?" She unbuttons her jacket and starts untucking her blouse. "Wondering what I was wearing underneath, weren't you?"

"Fucking always," I admit.

"Why don't you come find out?"

CHAPTER SEVENTEEN

OLIVIA

MAVERICK LOOKS at me with so much lust, I think I'll combust if he doesn't get inside me soon. I finish undressing to my bra and panties and watch as he makes a show of wiping the drool off his chin.

"I wish I had time to taste you right now, but that'll have to wait until later."

Later? I like the sound of that.

When he shoves his jeans and boxers halfway down his legs, and his massive erection bounces, it's so much bigger than I remember. Granted, it wasn't actually hard the last time I saw it but holy fuck. Maverick Kingston *is* the whole package.

"I think you're the one drooling now," he taunts, sliding his tongue up my chin and pressing a deep, heated kiss on my mouth.

"Well, you would be too if you saw how big you are," I tease. "I wish I had time to get on my knees and worship it like it deserves." I throw a version of his words back at him, but it's one million percent the truth.

I watch as Maverick reaches into his back pocket and grabs his wallet. He pulls out a condom and rolls it over his length. I've never had bathroom sex before—or sex outside the bedroom period—so I let him take the lead. He takes me by surprise when he leans in and slowly kisses me, cupping my cheek with one hand, then gently easing himself between my legs. I do my best to arch my hips with the awkward position I'm in, but my body quickly adjusts, and soon he's in so fucking deep, I'm panting and moaning with the best pleasure I've felt in my life.

He pulls back slightly before ramming back inside me. Everything between us is fire and electricity, and I almost beg for more. Maverick dips his head to my neck, feathering kisses along my jawline and shoulder as he increases his pace, making my world spin over and over again.

"Goddammit, Olivia...you're so fucking tight. You feel so good," he growls in my ear, squeezing my hip as he pins me harder against the counter and mirror. "Your pussy is fucking amazing."

"Don't stop, Maverick. God, yesssss..." My head falls back slightly, but his other hand catches it and brings our mouths back together.

"You need it, don't you, sweetheart?" he asks in a rugged, deep voice that has me panting for more.

I nod in response, and before I can ask what he's doing, he has me bent over the sink with my ass in the air and his cock deep inside me. His hand smacks against my ass once, twice, and then I'm moaning for more.

"That's it, baby. Arch that back for me." He slides his hand up my spine, pushing my shoulders lower and when he's satisfied, he grabs my hips and pulls me back on his dick. "I'm gonna go so fucking deep. Hang on."

Maverick's promise has me so wet that when he hits the right spot, I scream out his name and beg him to keep going. He pushes harder and faster, and soon I'm spiraling into oblivion. The buildup is fast and sudden, and when he reaches around my waist to rub my clit, it sends me over until my body is shaking with the biggest release I've ever had. I barely come down before he's sinking deeper into me and sending me off the edge once again.

"Oh my God, Maverick. I can't..." I pant, losing my breath as he chases his own orgasm.

"So close, baby...you feel so goddamn good. I don't want it to end," he admits, sliding his hand around my chest and squeezing my breast. "And fuck, your tits are amazing too. Go figure." I watch him in the mirror, and he's smirking at me.

"I bet you're dying to taste them," I tease, knowing when we're back at the hotel he'll take every opportunity to do just that.

"Fuck yes, I am."

I bite my lower lip just thinking about it and lower my eyes to where our bodies are connected in the reflection.

"Keep your eyes on me, Olivia. I want you to see what you do to me. What you've been doing to me. I want there to be no doubt in your mind." His words are so intense that my eyes are glued to his, and when his body finally goes rigid and shakes against mine, I watch him as he unravels inside me. His eyes squeeze tight, his jaw clenches, and his nails dig into my hips. It's fucking beautiful.

Maverick comes with a deep groan, and my body tightens around him as he fills me. Moments pass, and then he's pulling out and tossing the condom away.

"We better get out of here before someone catches us," he

instructs as we layer our clothes on. "Then I'm taking you to my room and worshipping you all over again."

My phone alarm goes off, waking me out of a deep sleep. I roll over to turn it off and smack hard into a wall.

"Argh," I groan, feeling the immediate headache coming on. I drank more last night than I ever have before. I'm gonna need to find some meds stat.

"Mornin', beautiful." Maverick's deep, sleepy voice echoes out, and my eyes immediately shoot open.

Last night was definitely *not* a dream.

Wrapping an arm around my shoulders, he pulls me tighter to his body. Memories of our time together flash through my mind as panic starts to weigh on my chest.

What the hell did I do? I could lose my job over this. Rachel was adamant about her rules, and I just bulldozed over them. If she finds out, my career is completely over. Not only would she fire me, but she wouldn't give me the recommendation I'd need to find another job.

I'd be screwed.

"I can hear your thoughts racing a million miles an hour. Talk to me, Olivia." Maverick's tone is somehow smooth and rough at the same time, almost as if he's expecting me to freak out.

"I should go to my room before Rachel finds out I'm not there." I scramble to the edge of the bed, but Maverick grabs my wrist and holds me in place until he shifts his body behind me.

"Baby, wait."

Baby? Oh my God.

"Maverick, I can't. This...shouldn't have happened. I'm going to lose my job, everything." I jerk out of his grip and stand, taking the sheet with me to wrap around myself. Our clothes are littered all over the floor.

"Not if she doesn't find out," he tells me, which almost makes me laugh. Rachel's like a Russian spy. She finds out everything she needs to know, and the guilt written all over my face will be as obvious as Maverick's six-pack abs.

Leaning down to pick up my shirt and pants, I eye my panties and bra and scoop them up next.

"It doesn't matter either way. You and I both know this was a one-night thing. You're going home today, and I'll be praying I still have a job when I fly back to Chicago."

We still have one event left this morning, so I can plaster on a smile and fake it until it's over. Thank God the tour is coming to an end.

"You're overthinking this," Maverick tries to tell me, and when I look up at him, he's sitting on the edge of the bed pulling up his boxer shorts.

"No, I wasn't thinking—*period*." Taking my clothes, I walk into the bathroom and get dressed. I look at myself in the mirror, and my jaw drops. Maverick left bite marks on my neck and chest, and my hair is the exact definition of sex hair. Quickly, I change and try to fix my hair and makeup.

I can't chance running into Rachel before I can take a shower.

As soon as I open the bathroom door, Maverick is standing in the doorway, blocking my way out.

"Olivia, stay. Take a shower, and we can talk after. You don't need to rush off," he says. His words and voice are so genuine; if this were any other situation, I'd even consider it.

"I'm going to shower and change for the event in my room, and there's nothing to discuss. Last night happened, and there's nothing we can do about it now."

"Do about it?" His voice goes higher. "So last night meant nothing to you?" He stands tall with his arms crossed over his chest. "Is that what you're telling me?"

"I'm saying…" I linger, finally walking past him to gather my phone and shoes. "Considering the precedence our boss set, it shouldn't have happened."

"Fuck that, Olivia. Quit worrying about your job and just admit what you actually feel for once."

"I have to go." I find my purse, slip my shoes on, and head toward the door. Before opening it, I pause. "Rachel's reading is at noon. Meet me down in the lobby in an hour so we can go."

"I'm aware of the schedule, Olivia," he replies harshly.

"Good, just reminding you." I glance over my shoulder and see the pained expression on his face, and it kills me. "Please remember to act like nothing happened. Rachel will notice if something's off between us."

"Shouldn't be a problem for me. You're the one running away."

I part my lips to say something but decide against it and make my way out of his room. Once I'm in the hallway, I exhale a deep breath, feeling the emotions piling on top as I push away my pain.

An hour later, I'm showered and ready to go. Rachel has

already texted me three times, and I'm trying to mentally prepare myself, so she doesn't suspect a thing, though I'm wondering if Maverick will be able to keep his word.

"Where's Maverick?" Rachel's voice booms behind me, and I jump. Her tone is short and cold.

"Uh," I start, feeling flustered.

"I just had to make a quick stop to the bathroom," Maverick chimes in before I can respond. I glance over and see he's wearing a big smile.

Today, Rachel will read the first six chapters of the first book in the Bayshore Coast series at a local Barnes & Noble. Afterward, she'll sign books that people bring or bought, and then the tour will be complete.

"Olivia," Maverick whispers next to me as we stand to the side. Rachel is standing behind a podium with her book reading to her audience.

"What?" I ask without facing him.

"We need to talk."

I look over my shoulder at him and frown. "There's nothing to discuss."

"Like hell there isn't," he whisper-shouts, causing a few people to look over at us.

I scold him with my eyes to keep it down. He grabs my elbow and pulls me with him as he walks to a secluded part of the bookstore behind some shelves.

"What do you think you're doing?" I whisper-shout back at him.

"I want to know why you're acting as if last night never happened. I know you feel what I feel, Olivia. You might have this preconceived notion that I'm some kind of man whore, but we've been dancing around each other since day one. We have a connection, and there's no denying it. You aren't just some chick I picked up at the bar, and I'm not some guy you randomly met. So tell me how you can just pretend there's nothing between us?"

I meet his dark eyes, and I see the sincerity in them. His voice is deep and low, and I hate how pained it sounds.

"You know as well as I do that we could never work out, so I'm not going to live in a fantasy world and pretend that it could. I told you I could lose my career over this, so excuse me for not announcing it to the world that we slept together!"

"So that means you're going to erase last night from your memory? That's what you want? To act like we never happened and pretend our feelings don't exist?" He steps closer, narrowing the gap between us. I can smell his cologne, and it smells so fucking good, I want to drown in it.

"We have to, Maverick. Otherwise, we're just going to hurt more. Don't you understand? If I let myself fall for you, I'll end up with a broken heart. I'm married to my job. You're building a career in LA. You don't fly, so it's not like we could easily see each other. Last night was amazing, okay? But it can't ever happen again."

"I know the cards are stacked against us, but I also know that if I let you walk away without putting everything out there, I'd regret it. Give us a chance." He cups my face and rubs the pad of his thumb along my cheek. I wish I could say the words he desperately wants to hear, but I just can't.

I inhale deeply, trying to hold back the tears. "I'm sorry, Maverick."

Stepping away, I walk back toward the reading without looking back.

Getting your heart broken is one thing, but breaking someone else's heart is torture.

CHAPTER EIGHTEEN

MAVERICK

TODAY IS SO FUCKING BITTERSWEET, but it feels like a black cloud is hanging over me. Soon, I'll be back in Los Angeles, and it will be the end of Olivia's and my road, which she reminded me of at the signing. It passed by in a blur. I faked a smile and laugh, but her words fucking destroyed me. Olivia, in her typical fashion, put up a brick wall, and she won't allow me through. I'm hurt, and I'm pissed, and I wish for once she would just stop with the act. The way she kissed me last night meant something. We weren't just fucking. It was more emotional than that, and when I looked into her eyes, I know she felt it. I refuse to allow her to deny it and deny me.

After the signing, I go up to my room and pace around, wondering what I'm going to say. This isn't over. The smell of her body still lingers in my room, and I've got to escape it before I drive myself crazy. I pack my shit, then go downstairs to wait before she feels the need to send me a reminder text. At the beginning of this trip, I was ready for it to be over, but now I don't want it to end. And I don't think she does either.

I sit on a bench by the front door and wait for her, and I can't seem to shake this feeling. It's almost like an elephant is sitting on my chest. The days have been passing by so quick, and tomorrow when I wake up without Olivia, things will be different. And I'm not so sure that's a good thing. I've never felt this way about someone before. She's so fucking special, and forcing myself to forget her would be one of the greatest regrets of my life.

She eventually makes it downstairs but barely looks my way. I follow her out to the car, and the strain between us practically smothers me. Once we're on the highway, I randomly glance over at her, and she's paying zero attention to me as if I don't even exist. The tension is so thick it could cut through steel, and I hate it. Regardless of all my attempts to talk to her, she's purposely ignoring me. Olivia has already blocked me out, and it pisses me off because our time together is limited. It's not supposed to be like this. We shared something so intimate, and by the way she's acting right now, she's already erased it from her memory.

She's buried herself in her work, something I've learned she does when she's trying to avoid me. With one swift movement, I snatch her planner and roll down the window. I know I've already threatened her with this once, but I'm more serious than ever.

"Maverick. I swear to everything holy that if you let go of that planner, I will never forgive you."

I hear the pages fluttering in the wind and can tell she's overly annoyed, but it's the first time I've held her attention all day. I pull the planner inside and throw it in the back seat. When she turns around to grab it, I place my palm on her face and force her to look at me. With everything I am, I try to keep my attention on the road, but she needs to hear what I have to say.

"Olivia. Just stop for five minutes, okay?" I look forward and notice we're heading straight into standstill traffic. Just what I need to tell her what I have to say. Once we're stopped, I let out a deep breath. Taillights go on for miles, and while it's annoying, I'm thankful for the extra time I'll get to spend with her, even if she isn't. There's always traffic crossing the border to California, and it could take anywhere from thirty minutes to three hours to get through it, and by the look on Olivia's face, I know she wasn't prepared for it. Considering I drive everywhere, I was well aware, and for the first time ever, I'm happy to be waiting.

"After I lost my dad, I promised myself I wouldn't live my life with regrets, and that's why I take so many risks. But I know that if we head back to LA and go our separate ways without me telling you exactly how I feel or hearing you admit that our night together meant something, then I'll drown in the what-could've-beens. Olivia, I like you, okay? Like *really* like you. And I think you like me too." I look at her, and her eyes soften.

"I'm sure you tell that to a lot of women," she tries to joke, but I don't crack a smile.

"I don't. That's the thing. You have this made-up version of me where I'm this playboy who just wines and dines all these women, and it's not true. There's not been anyone worth my time who has made me feel like this until you. Last night was something really fucking special. I'm not going to sit here and let you run from that. I refuse."

She swallows hard, and I watch as she tucks her bottom lip into her mouth. Gently, I place my thumb under her chin and lean forward, pulling that lip into my mouth and sucking on it. At first, she tenses, but not even she can deny how she truly feels. Olivia breaks down and kisses me back, pouring herself into me. Her tongue swipes against mine, and I want to devour her. As our kiss deepens, honking horns pull us apart, and we both laugh as I drive forward.

"If Rachel..."

"I don't give two shits about what Rachel thinks. We're consenting adults and can do whatever we want. It's not her business what anyone does behind closed doors, especially you. Stop letting her run your life outside of work. Stop using her as an excuse to run from your feelings, okay? I'm not ashamed of what happened, Olivia."

"I'm not either," she says, and I almost see her crack a smile.

"The difference between us is, I want the world to know how I feel about you, but you're okay with keeping me as a secret, tucked away to be forgotten as soon as you get on that plane to Chicago."

She shakes her head. "It's not like that, Maverick. I do have feelings for you, but we live a world apart. And who's to say, once we're not on the road, that things would even work out between us? I have my job and life in Chicago, and yours is in LA. So where does that leave us?"

Traffic begins to move more quickly, and soon we're crossing the border into California.

"It leaves us trying. Isn't what we have worth that, at least?"

She looks out the window, and I catch a glimpse of her reflection. Somber, it's the only way I can describe it. I don't push it any further, because I want to enjoy the time I have left with her. The clock is ticking, and with each passing second, I feel her slipping through my fingers.

Eventually, we make it to Los Angeles, two hours past when we were expected to arrive, which isn't surprising. I drive to my condo, and when I pull into the driveway, I look over at her.

"Well, I guess this is goodbye," she says, her tone flat.

I tuck a loose strand of hair behind her ear. "It doesn't have to be. Just one more night, Olivia. Please."

"But I have a hotel reserved already," she reminds me as if that matters. She's still trying to push me away, still trying to avoid what she's feeling. Her words can spew lies but her body can't.

I lean forward and whisper softly across her lips. "Cancel it." She parts her lips just slightly before closing her mouth again. "I'm only asking for one night. Say yes, Olivia." Her breath hitches before I close the gap between our lips.

"Okay," she says, breathlessly. "Yes."

The electricity streaming between us is so strong, I know she can't deny it. I turn off the car and pull the keys from the ignition. We both step out and grab our bags. I only asked her to stay one night, so this feels like a final goodbye, but I push the thoughts away. She grabs her laptop bag, but I take it from her hands and place it back in the trunk and shut it.

"Not tonight." I refuse to let her ignore me because of work.

She lets out a laugh. "I kinda like this side of you. Almost like a real-life Ian."

"Yeah? Well, hang on to your panties, sweetheart. There's more where that came from."

I punch in the code to my door, and we walk inside. She leaves her bags by the door and looks around.

"Shall I give you the grand tour?" I ask, smirking.

"I'd love one," Olivia replies with a grin. She follows me into the living room and looks at the photos of my family on the mantle. "This is your dad?"

I stand behind her and wrap my arms around her body, nodding. "Yeah. This is the plane we used for all our family trips."

"Wow. That would've been amazing." Her voice sounds so sweet.

"It was. Some of the best times of my life were in that plane."

She sets the picture down and picks up the next one. "This is your brother and sister?"

I glance at it, and we're all standing in front of a Christmas tree. "Yep. It was taken a few years ago."

"Holy shit! Is your entire family beautiful?" She laughs, glancing at the picture of my mom and all of us.

I set the picture down and spin her around until she's facing me, and I hold her close. "Are you hungry?"

"For you," she whispers. I pop an eyebrow at her before she stands on her tiptoes and steals a kiss.

"Hi there. My name is Maverick," I tease, and she playfully smacks my chest.

"If you introduce yourself to me one more time…" Olivia warns.

With one swift movement, I lift her into my arms.

She lets out a scream followed by a laugh as I walk us toward my bedroom. "Put me down!"

"No can do, sweetheart." I set her down on my bed. Blond hair cascades around her head, and at this moment, she's picture perfect. She props herself up on elbows and watches me as I unbutton my shirt. When it drops to the floor, she stands and walks toward me.

"Need some help?" she asks, unbuttoning my pants. I love it when she takes control, and I willingly allow her to.

I run my fingers through her hair and lean down to kiss her, wanting to inhale her—all of her. Pulling back, I peel her shirt off her body and toss it to the floor. My fingers brush across her soft skin as I reach around and undo her black lacy bra, causing goose bumps to surface.

"Fuck, Olivia. You're so beautiful." I lean down, taking her nipple in my mouth. Her head falls back on her shoulders as she runs her fingers through my hair.

"I need you," she whispers, and I smile as my lips memorize her body, loving her admission.

Carefully, I unzip her skirt and slide it down her body along with her pantyhose. She kicks off her heels, and I hook my fingers in her panties and help her step out of them. Olivia stands naked and confident, and I take a few seconds to soak in her flawless curves.

She reaches for me, scooting my boxers down my body and wraps her hand around my erection. A moan escapes me, and this only encourages her to continue stroking me. I'm putty in her hands, and she knows it.

Before I lose control, I move Olivia back to the bed. Her eyes flutter closed as I kiss up her calf, between her thighs, and find her sweet spot. Gasps and moans fill the room as my tongue twirls against her clit. Olivia rocks her hips against my mouth until her breathing increases.

"Not yet," I growl. She's a greedy little thing, and I love it. As I pull away, she releases an annoyed pant, and I chuckle, teasing her with flicks of my tongue. Pushing herself up on her elbows, she glares at me, which only causes me to burst out laughing.

"You're so damn sassy," I tell her.

"You're teasing the fuck out of me on purpose," she says with a sexy smirk. "Just wait. I'll get you back."

I hum against her clit, which only causes her to writhe against me. As she becomes greedier, I grab her ass cheeks and pull her closer to my mouth. I take all of her, licking and flicking and sucking her clit, watching her come undone beneath me. With arched hips, her body tenses, and within moments, she's losing herself against my tongue. I taste her, not wasting a drop as she rides her release.

Olivia is panting, her chest rapidly rising and falling, as I crawl onto the bed and hover above her. She leans up and kisses my lips, tasting herself.

Slowly, I enter her, filling her with my length. With sharp nails, she scratches down my back as I rock back and forth, enjoying the moment. We're slowly falling in the abyss together where the only thing that matters is us. Time makes no difference—only the right now. I need her as much as she needs me. We're two broken people mending together to create a whole, and I don't ever want to let her go.

Emotions roll through me, and it feels like an out-of-body experience as I look into her hooded eyes. Is it too soon to have these types of feelings for someone I met only two weeks ago? I could love her if she'd let me. If she'd tear down her walls and let me inside, I'd give her everything.

Her body tenses and tightens as her mouth ravages mine. Our tongues twist together, and there's nothing in the world that I want other than her.

"More," she demands. I increase my pace and ram into her harder, giving her exactly what she needs. Soon, she's bucking beneath me, screaming my name for all of LA to hear. The orgasm builds so quickly that soon, I'm losing control too. I feel as if I'm free-falling straight into Olivia's heart as she holds me tight against her warm, soft body. I wish we could stay here forever, but I know that's not an option in her eyes.

After we clean up, I pull her into my arms as she lays her head against my chest.

"I'm really going to miss you, Maverick."

It feels like the end, but I refuse to let it be. "I'm going to miss you, too, Miss Priss."

She lets out a laugh as she playfully slaps my chest. I kiss her on the forehead, and we lie together in silence. The past two weeks flash through my mind, from the moment we first met until now, and a smile fills my face.

Eventually, I fall asleep with Olivia in my arms, and I hold her as tight as I can, almost afraid she'll disappear if I let go.

I sleep without dreaming, and when the sun peeks through my curtains, I roll over and reach for her. My eyes flutter open, and I realize she's gone. The bed is cold where her body once was, and I'm hurt she didn't wake me before leaving, but then again, I know it might've been too hard to really say goodbye.

After everything we shared during our trip, I just don't know how I'll be able to move on from Olivia—or if I'll ever want to.

CHAPTER NINETEEN

OLIVIA

"I NEED a tuna salad wrap to go, please," I tell the cashier, pulling out my card. "And a skinny vanilla latte."

Once I pay and grab my order, I rush down the street in a maze through the crowd of people. With my messenger bag slung over my shoulder, carrying my planners and shoes, I'm jogging back to Rachel's house before she scolds me for being late. I've already been working on her next year's book signing tour among a dozen other tasks. It's only been a week since I returned from LA, but it already feels like a distant memory.

Except for Maverick.

Everything about him is front and center in my mind. The way he smells, the taste of his lips, the sound of his laughter...

He texted me the day after I left to make sure I made it home safely. After I told him I did and thanked him for checking on me, I apologized for not saying goodbye because I didn't want to wake him so early. It wasn't a complete lie, but I also couldn't stand to see that hurt look in his eyes. I also knew if I had to say goodbye, I might change my mind. I couldn't risk hurting him.

Maverick said he understood and hoped we'd keep in touch.

I didn't text him back after that.

"Here you devil," I whisper, throwing Angel her treat so she won't bark at me as soon as I walk into the apartment.

I walk into Rachel's office, set her food and coffee down, then head back to my desk and start going over my to-do list.

When I'm finally able to check my phone, I see two new messages from Maverick. I don't know why I feel all giddy inside from just seeing his name on my screen, but my heart is racing as I anticipate what he said.

Maverick: Do you think my spray tan is too dark? I have a photo shoot tomorrow.

The next message is a picture of him holding up his shirt and showing off his too-perfect abs. I snort and shake my head at his obnoxiousness.

Olivia: Considering you're only showing a small part of your body, it's too hard to tell.

Maverick: Fair point. Hold on.

Oh God. What does that mean? He's not going to send me a nude, is he?

Would I want him to?

Maverick: What about now?

He then sends me a picture of a mirror shot of his backside, *naked*. Bare ass and all.

Olivia: Are you going to be showing that part of your body in the shoot?

Maverick: No. But I got a full body spray tan, so my question still stands.

I swallow, thinking how to respond. This is the playful side of Maverick I enjoy. Granted, he was usually poking fun at me, but I can't deny that he made that road trip an experience I'll never forget.

Olivia: I think it looks satisfactory. No complaints.

Maverick: Satisfactory? Okay, thanks, Grandma.

Olivia: What? It looks great. There, better? I've never had someone show me their ass before to ask how their tan was, so forgive me.

Maverick: Apology accepted.

Olivia: So wait. You do spray tans naked? Like naked naked?

Maverick: Yep. Even my dick has a nice tan. Wanna see?

Olivia: No! Don't you dare send me a dick pic.

Maverick: Oh yeah, forgot you're a prude. Better delete my abs and ass picture just in case ;)

Olivia: Why do you live to torture me?

Maverick: I got so used to doing it every day, and now I'm going through withdrawals.

Olivia: Funny.

Maverick: I try. So how's it been back to work in the office? Missing my rock 'n' roll music, aren't you?

Olivia: Torture as always. Rachel's on my ass about everything, so nothing new. No actually. It's been stuck in my head for days, though.

Maverick: It's washing out your classical sleepy crap.

Olivia: I beg to differ.

Maverick: I like it when you beg.

Olivia: Maverick. Don't.

Maverick: If I recall when I had you bent over, it was "Maverick, don't stop."

Olivia: I'm going to smack you.

The next message is the same picture of his ass except now it's zoomed in.

Maverick: I'll be ready for it.

"Olivia!" Rachel's voice snaps me away from my phone, and she looks like she's about to pop a blood vessel. "Can you get me that email now?"

"Yes. Yes, of course." I scramble to my laptop and search for the email she told me she wanted earlier. I can't get the stupid, goofy grin off my face thinking about Maverick and his text messages. I can even hear his voice reading them, and it has me blushing all over again. "Just sent it to you."

"Pay attention next time, please."

You're welcome, I'm tempted to say but keep my mouth tight-lipped. Saying the words thank you might actually damage her throat.

I finish the day with an achy back and sore feet as usual, but I wait until I'm home to take off my shoes. Deciding to take a bath, I start stripping my clothes as I walk to the bathroom and turn on the water. I glance down at my phone to check the time and set it on the edge of the tub. It's been such a long week. Rachel has me working even longer days, so I've had zero time to recover since returning from the tour. I wish she would've given me a few days off, but that'd be too convenient.

Just as I'm sliding into my tub, I hear my phone ding, and my stomach flutters with anticipation. I didn't have a chance to reply to Maverick's last message, and I'm not convinced texting is a good idea, considering our feelings for each other.

Regardless, I grab the phone and smile when I see his name.

Maverick: What are you doing right now?

Deciding to mess with him, I send him a snapshot of my feet poking out of the bathwater.

Maverick: Are you seriously in the tub right now?

Olivia: Yep. Long day. Everything hurts.

Maverick: So you're naked?

I chuckle, knowing he's focusing hard on that very fact right now.

Olivia: That's typically how you take a bath.

Maverick: And I'm sorry you had a long, hard day. I'd rub your muscles for you if I could.

Olivia: I'm sure that's all you'd do.

Maverick: Well, I was trying to be a gentleman, but if you want to know the truth...

I bite my lip and send him another text.

Olivia: Okay, tell me...

Maverick: I'd give you a full body massage with

some scented oils and make sure to cover every inch of your incredible body. I have big, strong hands, so you'd be moaning and begging for more —of the massage, I mean. I'd rub out all your knots and take care of all your soreness. Then I'd flip you to your back and take care of all your other needs.

Fuck, that sounds like heaven. I could really use all that right now.

Olivia: I like the sound of that. Too bad you're like a million miles away.

Maverick: That doesn't mean I can't help you relax in other ways.

Olivia: Oh yeah? Enlighten me.

Maverick: Slide your hand between your thighs.

Olivia: Are you serious?

Maverick: Do it, Olivia. Don't you trust me?

I sigh.

Olivia: Of course, I do.

Maverick: Then tell me how tight you feel. Slide your fingers inside. Are you wet?

Olivia: I'm in the bathtub. My whole body is wet.

Maverick: Funny.

Olivia: I thought so. *shrugs* Fine.

Maverick: Rub your clit.

Olivia: I am. It's really sensitive tonight.

Maverick: Good. I wish I could suck on it. Taste you. Slide my tongue inside your pussy and feel your body tighten around me.

Holy shit. How are his words making me so incredibly hot? Is this sexting? How does Maverick make me feel so damn comfortable in just a matter of hours? It's like no time has gone by, and we are right back to where we were before our awkward last day together.

Olivia: I'd like that, too.

Maverick: I know you would, sweetheart. But for now, just picture I'm there with you. Imagine it's my fingers inside you, fucking you and making you scream.

Oh God. Yes, I want alllll of that.

Olivia: I'm close, Maverick. My body is begging for it.

Maverick: Let go, baby. I'm right there with you.

My breathing picks up, and as I picture his hands and lips on me, I increase my pace until I'm riding a wave of intense pleasure. *Fuck*. That was definitely needed.

Olivia: Thank you.

Maverick: Are you seriously thanking me right now?

Olivia: Yes. Thank you for helping me relax.

Maverick: LOL... it was my pleasure. Let me know if I can help you with anything else.

Olivia: I'll talk to you later, Maverick. Good night.

Maverick: Night, Olivia.

That night, I go to bed feeling more relaxed than I have in months and with a big, stupid smile on my face.

Maverick: I can't believe you watch this crap.

Olivia: It's my guilty pleasure. Shut up.

Maverick: Kendall is seriously the dumbest chick I've ever seen. Cooper is a tool for even hooking up with her. This whole setup is crazy.

I can't help the smile on my face knowing Maverick is watching *Bachelor in Paradise* with me even though he claims to hate it. He secretly enjoys it, though he'll never admit it. This has been our Sunday night tradition for the past few weeks. We text during commercials, and he tells me how annoying everyone is.

Olivia: That's why it's called a guilty pleasure. Reality TV is always crazy! That's how they get their views.

Maverick: Well, it's killing brain cells. Also, Kendall's tits are totally fake.

Olivia: Obviously. They don't even bounce. That's how you know.

Maverick: They probably feel like bags of rocks.

Olivia: You'd probably know.

Maverick: Yours felt real to me. *Shrugs*

Olivia: Not me, asshole! Isn't LA full of fake boobs and nose jobs?

Maverick: Stereotypical.

Olivia: Not when I'm right.

Maverick: Isn't Chicago full of gangsters and sugar daddies?

Olivia: That sounds mostly right, though technically it's home to the best pizza in the world. Have you ever tried Chicago-style pizza?

Maverick: I have in LA, but I'm sure you're going to say it's not the same?

Olivia: Hell no! You need to experience it for real. In Chicago.

Maverick: Maybe someday.

Maybe someday. I know what that means.

It makes me sad when I think about how we'll probably never see each other face-to-face again. I don't plan to fly to LA anytime soon, and unless he plans to drive almost forty hours to Chicago, this is all we'll ever have. Even though it hurts to know that, I'd rather have his friendship like this than nothing at all. It's nice having someone to talk to who isn't barking orders at me all day long.

Olivia: I'd like that. OMG, Kendall just kissed Josh? WTF?

Maverick: Told you. She sucks.

Olivia: Hahaha... yeah she does.

Maverick: You owe me twenty bucks now!

Olivia: Ugh. Now you suck.

Maverick: Pay up, baby.

We make a bet every episode on who's going to "cheat" on their love interest, and I've lost every single week.

Olivia: How about I pay you another way?

Maverick: ...I'm listening.

Olivia: Take off your pants.

Maverick: It's cute you thought I was wearing pants this whole time.

Olivia: Argh. You ruined it.

Maverick: You're even more adorable when you get all flustered.

Olivia: I'm just gonna send you the money.

Maverick: LOL... there's my uptight city girl. I'm in my boxers... tell me what to do next.

Olivia: I want you to show me.

Maverick: I'm sorry. Have we met? I'm Maverick. And you are?

Olivia: Not funny.

Maverick: I'm laughing my ass off, so I beg to differ. Also, dick pic coming at you.

Olivia: Maverick, wait!

Too late.
And there he is in all his thick, hard glory.
I swallow then lick my lips, wishing I hadn't seen it.
Actually, that's a lie. I want all of it.

CHAPTER TWENTY

TEXTING with Olivia has been the only thing keeping me going since she left. I'm not much of a texter, but I can't get enough of it with her, and I look forward to it every day. I know she told me things could never work out between us, but these past few weeks have me hanging on to the hope that she'll change her mind and we'll figure something out together.

Between shoots and trying to keep up with my emails, I check in with her to make sure she's having a good day, and I look forward to making her smile or laugh at night when it's just the two of us. I don't even mind watching her ridiculous TV shows if it means we have something fun to talk about.

Maverick: I had a dream about you last night. You were wearing a naughty nurse outfit.

Olivia: Was it Halloween?

Maverick: Nope.

Olivia: Then it was definitely a dream.

Maverick: A dirty fantasy.

Olivia: Keep dreaming, playboy.

Maverick: You're the star in all my dreams, so if I drift off…

Olivia: You're relentless.

Maverick: It's why you like me.

Olivia: Debatable.

Maverick: So I have a shoot this afternoon. Do you want to FaceTime after?

We've only strictly texted up to this point, but I want to see her face. I miss the cute little quirky expressions she makes. The way she bites her lip, wrinkles her nose, and scolds me with narrowed eyes. I wouldn't mind seeing her O face again either.

Olivia: Um… maybe.

Maverick: C'mon, Olivia. Don't you miss my adorable face?

Olivia: No, because it's normally talking and saying arrogant things like that.

Maverick: Can't turn the charm off, baby.

Olivia: So I've heard. What time do you want to chat tonight?

Maverick: How's 6 your time?

Olivia: I'll be here.

I smile victoriously when she finally agrees. I've loved texting back and forth with her, but nothing compares to actually seeing her gorgeous face. Olivia Carpenter is my girl, and I'm going to do whatever's possible to prove it to her.

"Maverick, shirt and jeans off. Mess up your hair a bit too," Jeannie orders five seconds after I walk into the studio.

"What? Not gonna even buy me dinner first?"

"Cute. I have thirty minutes, Mav." She waves a finger at me to start stripping.

I've done several shoots with Jeannie before, so I enjoy messing with her and getting her worked up. She's doing new shots for me so my agent can send them to agencies for magazines for their winter issues. I'd really love to be able to do another campaign for Calvin Klein or Levi's again, but that's part of the job. I'm never sure when my next gig will be, so I just keep going, hoping someone picks me up.

"Great, let's do some head shots. Put a shirt on and give me your best smolder," she directs after twenty minutes of full body shots in various angles and positions.

She reminds me a little of Olivia. Blunt and direct. Always to the point. It's so much hotter when it comes from Olivia, though.

Once we're done, I thank her and head out. I'm dying to talk to Olivia again. I've never been this lovesick over a woman before, but I know she isn't just "some girl."

Maverick: I'm gonna grab something to eat and then I'll be ready to chat. You?

I watch as the dots jump on the screen as she replies, but then it stops. Finally, a minute passes, and she replies.

Olivia: Sure, I can make that work.

Something feels off, and I'm not sure what it is, but either way, I'm excited. Not seeing her after a month has been way too damn long.

Maverick: You should eat with me. Are you hungry?

Olivia: What are you talking about?

Maverick: I want to eat with you. Have you had dinner yet?

Olivia: No. Been running around for Rachel all day. Just about to walk into my apartment.

Maverick: Perfect. Change into something comfortable, and I'll take care of dinner.

Olivia: Wait. What?

Maverick: Do you trust me?

Olivia: *Sigh* Yes. Fine.

Maverick: Good. I'll call you in twenty.

I do some Google searches on my phone and am soon placing an order for delivery. She never lets anyone take care of her, and I'm about to change that.

Before I head home, I pick up an order of Chinese food, and once I get the notification that Olivia's food has been delivered, I grab my laptop and call her.

"Hey," she answers with a smug grin. "You didn't have to do that."

"I wanted to. Plus, I knew you'd skip dinner if I didn't feed you," I reply, holding my plate up for her to see. "And now we can eat Chinese together."

"It's delicious. If you weren't watching me, I'd be stuffing my face right now." She chuckles, getting comfortable on her couch with a plateful of food.

"Uh, when has that ever stopped you before? I've seen you inhale a bacon double cheeseburger."

She laughs, and the sound is like music to my ears. "To be fair, that was a damn good burger."

"I love seeing you smile, Olivia. I've missed it," I tell her sincerely.

"It's definitely been a long time since I've felt like smiling. Rachel just finished going through the plotting and outlining phase, so she's not sleeping much, which makes my job even more hell than usual. She even called on my day off to ask if I knew where her coffee filters were. THEY WERE LITER-ALLY ON TOP OF THE COFFEEMAKER," she shouts, but the face she makes with it has me bending over laughing my ass off.

"Tell me why you put up with her again?" I ask, genuinely wanting to know. Olivia is amazing, and I hate that she gets treated like scum. "You're smart, babe. You could run your own PR marketing company."

She looks down and shrugs. "I know she means well. I can't afford not to have a job, and the pay is great. Rachel even offers full benefits and holiday pay. That's a hard thing to walk away from. I'd love to start my own company, but I'd never have enough to cover the start-up costs."

"Plenty of new business owners take out loans for that type of thing. I think you should do it. You have so much knowledge about publishing and that whole community that you'd have clients in no time. Then you'd have to start hiring people to help with the workload. I can see it now." I flash her a bright smile, wanting her to know I mean every word.

"I don't know," she says reluctantly, moving the food around on her plate. "That sounds wonderful in theory, but there's a lot of competition for that. There's a lot of reputable PR companies already out there who are established. I'd be a small fish in a huge pond."

"You're preaching to the choir, babe. I'm a model. Living in LA. Could I be any more cliché?"

That makes her laugh, and she agrees with a nod.

"How's your food? Is it as good as mine?" I ask, changing the subject to ease the tension.

"It's quite delicious. You picked good."

"I'm glad you approve."

"I was ready to beat the delivery driver with a plastic bat. No one ever knocks on my door," she tells me.

"And you were going to protect yourself with a kid's baseball bat?" I ask, chuckling in amusement.

"It was all I could find! Someone knocking on my door unexpectedly spooked me."

"You're adorable," I say, staring at her. I know she hates compliments like that, but I can't help it. I miss her so damn much. "So any plans for another trip soon?"

"Not until next year. She has this new series planned, and her publisher is going nuts over it. They want to send her all over and even to Canada. There's even been talk about her going to Germany and France."

"Wow...that's a big step from our road trip."

"Uh, yeah. Rachel lives for the high life. She'll probably complain the entire time but secretly love it. I'm clearly looking so forward to it." She rolls her eyes just like I've come to adore.

"I wish you were closer."

"I know. We already went down that road, Maverick. I live here, and you live there."

"But I want you here," I tell her, pouting out my lower lip. "It's warm and sunny year-round. We have the best food trucks, and as added bonus, I'm here." I wink at her, and she gives me a dramatic sigh.

"I like talking to you, Maverick. When you aren't threatening to throw my planner out the window or taunting me with your abs, I consider you one of my closest friends. Hell, aside from Vada, you're really my only friend. But that's all I can offer. You know this." Her words are soft and tender, but that doesn't stop it from feeling like a knife just pierced through my heart.

"A friend? I think you and I both know we're more than friends. You should know I want more with you. After waking up without you in my bed, I knew my heart was already yours. I'd never cared about a chick bailing on me. It was the first time I felt heartache. I understood why you did it, but it didn't stop it from hurting."

"Maverick…" She says my name with a sad tone. "Perhaps we should've just left whatever this is in LA. You're only going to get hurt again."

"I don't want to just forget everything that happened between us. If text messages and FaceTime is all we can ever have, then I'll take it. I'll take whatever you give me," I tell her, hoping like hell she'll say she can at least do that. I knew long distance would be hard, but I'm not giving up without a fight. "I'm falling for you, Olivia."

"Maverick—I'm sorry. I can't." She tilts her head back and looks up at the ceiling as if she's trying to keep herself from crying. I hate how upset she looks. I just want to hold her in my arms and never let go. "It's too painful for me. I'm sorry."

Before I can reply, she disconnects, and I'm left with a black screen.

I'm not giving up on her. *I won't.*

It's been three days since Olivia and I last talked, and I'm going insane.

She won't reply to my text messages or answer my phone calls. I've left her voicemails, apologizing for pushing her too hard and that I'll respect her decision to keep us where we are—even if it kills me—but she hasn't called back.

Telling her I've fallen for her wasn't a lie—by any means—but perhaps she wasn't ready to hear it. Hell, maybe it scared her because she's fallen for me too.

Whatever her reasoning, I wish she'd give me a chance to fix it—fix *us*. I just want to talk to her, hear her voice, and see her beautiful face.

Maverick: Good morning, gorgeous. I hope you have a great day today.

Considering she didn't reply to my last eight text messages, I don't anticipate she'll respond to this one either. However, that doesn't stop me from sending them with hopes to brighten her day, because I know she's reading them.

Maverick: Good night, baby. I hope you get a great night's sleep.

I know she's pushing me away, thinking it's the best for both of us, but she's wrong. She's trying to control everything, and this time, I'm not going to allow it.

CHAPTER TWENTY-ONE

OLIVIA

IT'S the first time Maverick has visited my dreams since I stopped answering his texts and calls. Last week, I realized that I was falling way too hard—and he told me he was falling for me—and he'd become an integral part of my day. Things were moving in a direction that would only lead to heartbreak, and it was best to cut ties before things got even more complicated. My heart still flutters when I think about him, and that's frightening as hell.

I thought maybe my subconscious was mad at me for cutting him off, but then it presented me with the hottest sex dream I've ever had. I force myself out of bed and take a cold shower to rid my thoughts of him.

I know the statistics for long-distance relationships. Forty percent break up, and out of that, the split happens within the first four months—after the honeymoon phase and the real work begins. I care about him so damn much, but this is the best decision for both of us. He deserves someone who can give him what he wants and needs. Someone who doesn't live across the country, isn't married to their job, and can emotionally give him the relationship he deserves. I hate that I can't be that for him, and he might not agree with my reasoning, but I know it's for the best in the long run.

As I'm drying off, I hear my phone buzzing, and by the number of texts I'm receiving at once, I know it's Rachel having one of her early morning meltdowns. Not sure if I'm prepared for it today. I wrap the towel around my body, walk into my bedroom, and grab my phone from the nightstand.

Rachel: I ran out of my vegan protein powder. Can you stop and grab some before coming this morning?

Rachel: The health store across town opens at 7AM.

Rachel: Vanilla bean. If they don't have that, then chocolate will do.

Rachel: Can you pick up some of those cookies & cream protein bars too?

Rachel: Make sure to keep the receipt.

Rachel: And be quick.

I roll my eyes and shake my head as my hair drips water down my body. It's not even seven yet, and of course, there are no courtesy words used—please or thank you.

I need a truckload of caffeine before I can deal with her this morning.

Instead of replying, I send her a thumbs-up emoji

because I don't trust myself with words yet. The way I really feel might leak out this early which would result in me being fired and left high and dry without a reference. Not that the job market is booming with positions anyway.

I walk to the kitchen and start a pot of coffee, because I forgot to schedule it last night, then get dressed. The sun leaks through my curtains, and I smile as it splashes across the floor. Considering winter will be here in a blink, I try to soak up as much of it as I can. It's going to be another beautiful day, one where I'm stuck inside listening to Rachel bitch and moan about how hard her life is. Her life isn't hard—she's living the dream—but she's spoiled as hell and doesn't appreciate much.

Once the coffee is finished brewing, I pour a cup, add some French vanilla creamer, and take a sip. Before I can swallow, my phone starts vibrating again.

"Holy fuck," I whisper under my breath, hoping she doesn't send me on a scavenger hunt for a list of other things she wants because that's happened before.

I snatch my phone off my bed, but when I see it's texts from Maverick, my heart races.

Maverick: Good morning, gorgeous. Couldn't sleep. Thinking about you.

Maverick: Still ignoring me? :)

Guilt rushes through me, and I can't help but think I've led him on, that maybe he really thought this would progress into something more when he first texted me after our trip was over. Deep inside, I knew it wouldn't. It can't. Our lives are in two different places.

Maverick quickly became so much more to me than even he knows, and that scares the fuck out of me. Falling too fast and too hard reminds me too much of my mother, and I'll do anything I can to avoid that. Thankfully, we're thousands of miles apart, so it makes it slightly easier because he's not just going to show up on my doorstep, though it still hurts. This is exactly what I was afraid of from the beginning when our relationship began shifting. Ending it was the wisest and most logical decision.

Instead of replying, like I want to, I close out of my messages and open my Uber app to schedule a car. I haven't responded to any of his texts, and a part of me wonders how long he's going to keep this up. He's setting himself up for heartache, and it kills me in the process. His messages are what keep me going through the day, and even though I'm a total ass for not replying, I know that if I do, it'll just start a constant texting back and forth situation again.

Even though Rachel is a pain in my ass most days, I'm happy for the distraction today because my heart hurts. If I could, I'd stay locked up in my apartment and binge watch Netflix and eat ice cream. All while feeling sorry for myself. But I won't do that. I can't let myself go down that self-loathing path.

When my ride is close, I grab my laptop bag and head downstairs to wait. Once I'm inside the car, we head across town toward the health food store. I rush inside and grab the shit Rachel wants, say a little thank-you prayer for them having vanilla bean, then head back to my ride, who graciously waited.

On the way over to her apartment building, I feel a pressure weighing on me. I stare out the window and watch the people walk by on the street and can't help but wonder about their lives. Are they happy? In love? Sad? The Uber slows in front of Rachel's, and I thank him, grab my laptop bag, then head upstairs. The elevator is waiting, as always, and I give Sam a small smile, and that's when I realize I left Rachel's stupid protein powder in the car.

"Holy shit," I yell out and rush off the elevator toward the street. By the time I make it outside, the car is long gone. I stand on the sidewalk, pinching the bridge of my nose, trying to suck in air before I lose it. Like clockwork, my phone vibrates.

Rachel: Where are you? What's taking you so long?

I don't even know what to say.

Oh, I'm downstairs because I'm too busy daydreaming than paying attention?

Sure. That will go over really well, and I don't think I can handle being told to pay attention to detail today. Instead of saying anything yet, I open my Uber app and report a lost item, put my phone number in, and pace back and forth on the sidewalk as I wait for a return phone call. If this is an indication of how the rest of my day will go, I'm totally fucked.

My phone vibrates, and I'm so happy I might cry when I answer it and hear my driver's voice. After I explain what happened, he finds my plastic bag in the back seat and lets me know he's about ten minutes away. Relief floods through me. I might live to work another day. After I've got a solid timeline, I text Rachel back.

Olivia: I'll be there in about fifteen minutes.

Rachel: Why?

I let out a breath and suck in another one. Luckily, she's not the only one good with words.

Olivia: Just waiting on my Uber.

It's not the whole truth, but it's close enough to make her happy, or rather, make her not text me with any more questions. Soon I see the Toyota Corolla pulling up. The man hands me my stuff, and I give him a twenty because he saved my sanity. He tries to hand the money back, but I insist with a smile. My day might be shitty, but hopefully, his isn't.

I finally breathe when I'm back on in the lobby. Sam looks at me.

"Rough day, already?" He half-grins, then glances at his watch.

All I can do is smile. They all know Rachel is an absolute terror.

"Good luck," he says sweetly as the elevator doors slide open.

I step in and nod. "I'll need it."

Quickly, I pull my keys from my bag and step inside her apartment. I smell coffee and see Angel eating in the kitchen. Before Rachel can even ask, I prepare a protein shake and deliver it to her in her office. She's typing away and stops and looks up at me when I set it down with a smile.

"I need you to meet with Presley today since she's in town. We had a meeting last week, and I forgot to get copies of my contracts. You know exactly how I feel about that."

I nod. She's such a freak and doesn't trust scanned copies

of anything. She wants all originals. It's not the first time I've had to chase them down.

"I also made a grocery list, so I need you to hit the store on your way back. Then go to the post office and mail out last month's signed paperback giveaways for my reader group and check my PO Box."

I bite the inside of my mouth, and I might actually taste blood when I see a hundred signed books that need to be individually packaged and mailed. "Sure."

"Presley will be at her studio around ten. So." That's her passive-aggressive way of telling me I need to hurry. Just as I walk over to the books to get started, she takes a sip of her protein shake and practically spits it out.

"Oh my God, Olivia. Did you put any banana in here? This tastes like shit!" Rachel stands, snatches the protein shake from her desk, and storms into the kitchen like a two-year-old who got milk instead of juice. The blender goes off, and I know she's remaking it. One day, she's eating bananas, and the next, she's not. How the hell am I supposed to know when those carbs are okay?

While she's busy making her point in the kitchen, I open my laptop, connect to the wireless printer, and try to make some order out of her madness. Books are signed, and I'm forced to open each one to figure out who it's personalized to and try to find the person's address on the list. Clusterfuck doesn't give this catastrophe justice, and I have two hours to make it happen.

After the first hour, my back hurts so bad from bending over to stuff envelopes with books and postcards. By some miracle, I figure it out. Close to the two-hour mark, everything is packaged, labeled, and placed in huge totes for me to take to the post office. If she would've thought of this yesterday, I could've scheduled a pickup, but I'm pretty sure "inconvenience" is her middle name. It takes me four trips to carry everything to the bottom floor, and thankfully, Sam helps me as I schedule a ride.

Before my Uber arrives, Rachel texts me her grocery list, and if I didn't know better, I'd say she's stocking up for the winter because there's no way one person can eat all of this. The car pulls up, and the driver gets out and helps me load the totes into the trunk.

"Jesus, what're in these bags? Bricks?" She laughs.

"Close. Books," I say as I climb into the back and we take off. Instead of having the driver wait around for me, I let her leave because the line at the post office is longer than I anticipated. Rachel insists she get the receipt that shows they've been mailed, so instead of just dropping them in the cart, I'm forced to wait.

After an hour, the packages are finally mailed, the PO Box is checked, and I'm scheduling a ride across town toward Presley's rented studio. I try to cheer up because I really like Presley, but I'm in such a sour mood that I'm not sure I can shake it. She's dealt with Rachel for the past five years, so I know she understands my frustration.

I'm dropped off in front of a brick building with large windows. There's nothing too fancy about the outside of it, but the inside is gorgeous. There's a backdrop set up in one area, hardwood floors, and the most perfect natural lighting. The space was made for photo shoots, especially with her eye. She's one of the most creative people I know.

As soon as I walk in, I tuck Rachel's fan mail under my arm. Presley peeks up from her makeshift office space with a smile. "Hey, you!"

I let out a breath, and it's the first time today since

Maverick's text this morning that I've genuinely smiled. The heels of my shoes click against the wood floor as I walk toward her.

"You look like hell," she says when I move closer.

I narrow my eyes at her. "Do I even have to explain why?"

She snorts. "No. It's because you work for the devil incarnate." Presley can barely get her words out before laughing.

Though I want to join in on bashing Rachel, I don't because it's too easy. "Where're the fingerprints, blood samples, and DNA results?"

Presley stands and grabs a manila folder. I open it and see the original signed contracts, and I hold on to them tightly. If I lose these, it will be my head.

"Have you eaten lunch yet?" she asks. "It's about that time." She looks down at her watch and grins at me.

Shaking my head, I smirk. "There's no time for food, Pres. I still have to go grocery shopping. Though, with the list she gave me, it might just be easier to buy the whole store."

"No offense against you, but I'm actually surprised you've lasted this long with her. You're her assistant, not her maid, housekeeper, or dog sitter. I hate to say it, but you need to set some boundaries. If not, she's going to continue to walk all over you because you've allowed it for so long."

She's right. I know she's right. Maverick even said the same thing. However, I need this job like I need air. "I know." Glancing down at my phone, I realize I've already wasted too much time.

Presley stands and gives me a big hug and a smile. "I'm sorry."

Pulling back, I narrow my eyes at her. "For what?"

A door closes in the studio, and I hear footsteps on the wooden floor behind me. I turn around to see who's coming, and when my eyes meet Maverick's, I feel as if I'm falling. Quickly, I turn and glare at Presley who shrugs and goes back to her computer. "Told you I was sorry."

"How did you know?" I whisper, wondering how she knew about Maverick and me. Seeing him standing so damn sexy, wearing clothes that hug him in all the right places, makes me forget every reason I've been avoiding him. The need I have for him is too damn powerful to ignore.

She just grins. "I have my resources."

CHAPTER TWENTY-TWO

MAVERICK

THE MOMENT my eyes meet hers, it's as if time stands stills. She's just as beautiful as the last time I saw her. My heart lurches forward, and though my feet feel frozen to the floor, I force myself to walk toward her. The fact that she's shocked, with her jaw dropped, makes not telling her I'd be here worth it. I wanted to surprise her but wasn't sure if this would be a good or bad surprise, considering she hasn't been talking to me. Distance is hard, but for her, I'd try anything. The only way to tell her how I really feel is in person.

"Maverick. What are you doing here?" she finally asks, blinking hard as if to make sure I'm real.

I don't immediately answer, and Presley raises her hand, temporarily bringing the attention back to her. "I booked him for a shoot. Wanted to show him around the studio first." By the look on Presley's face, I know she's bluffing. She must know about our history and planned this somehow.

Olivia turns and looks at Presley, shaking her head. All I want to do is pull her into my arms and kiss the fuck out of her, but I know Olivia prefers discretion and privacy. I'm not one to kiss and tell, mainly because Olivia doesn't want anyone to know. The truth is, I don't want Olivia to be my best-kept secret. I want the fucking world to know how I feel.

"Surprise?" I smirk with a shrug, hoping she doesn't push me away again. I don't know if I could handle being rejected by her in person.

As she walks forward, her heels click on the wood floor. "Surprise? Surprise?! You're in Chicago. Here. Right now. And that's all you have to say?"

I nod and close the gap between us. She places her hands on her hips, giving me all sorts of sass, and I pull her into my arms. Though Olivia is reserved, and Presley is around, I don't care. I can't wait any longer. Ever since I signed the contracts for the shoot, I've been thinking about this very moment, what I would say to her when we were face-to-face and how this would all play out. I just didn't expect her to be here when I arrived, so I'm somewhat shocked as well. Divine intervention wins again.

Not another minute can pass without me knowing if my feelings will be reciprocated. There's no rushing when I pull her close. My lips softly press against hers, and she sinks into me, the kiss growing deeper. It's as if no time has passed at all, and I'm so damn happy that when we pull apart, a grin fills her face.

Olivia reaches back and smacks my arm.

"Hey!" I playfully say, rubbing the area as if it actually hurt.

"You deserve that!" she responds.

"Why?" I chuckle. "You're the one who's been ignoring me."

Presley stands, smiles, and then makes her way across

the studio. "I'll see you two lovebirds later," she announces, and then I hear the door click closed.

As soon as she's out of sight, Olivia wraps her arms around my waist. "I'm really glad you're here. I know I have a lot of explaining to do."

"Have you eaten yet?" I ask, knowing she probably hasn't.

Before she can respond, her phone goes off. She groans as she pulls it from her pocket. "Shit. I have to go. I'm so sorry. I still need to go grocery shopping for Rachel and work for a few more hours before I'm released from prison. Will you be around later?"

I take her phone from her hand. "Rachel can wait. We're having lunch."

She opens her mouth to argue, but I place my finger over her lips. "Say yes, Olivia."

"You know I can't deny you when you look at me like that," she admits with a pouty face.

"Like what, like you're a delicate flower?" I laugh, reminding her what Rachel once said. Instantly, Olivia rolls her eyes.

"Okay, fine. Lunch. Then I really have to get back to work."

I smirk. "I'll take what I can get."

We walk outside, and Olivia bursts out into laughter when she sees the Toyota Prius parked on the street.

"Are you kidding me? I thought you didn't do Prius?" she asks with her hands placed on her hips.

"They don't bother me that much. I just wanted to see how far I could push you. I won, didn't I?" I unlock the car and walk toward it.

"You asshole!" She chuckles getting inside. "Do you have any idea what I had to do to get rid of that car in LA?"

"Sell your kidney?" I glance over at her, and it almost feels like we're getting ready for another adventure, and in a way, we are.

"Basically. I promised my firstborn and had to slip the guy a fifty."

When I laugh, she scolds me for being a douche when we first met. I almost apologize, but then don't, because I don't regret anything that led us to where we are right now.

"Where do you want to eat?" I ask, pulling out onto the street.

"Chicago pizza. The real kind, not that bullshit you eat in LA." She glances at me, and I see the blush hit her cheeks.

"Perfect." I let her plug in the address and have the GPS guide me. After we park and get out, I place my hand on the small of her back as we walk in. She looks over at me and smiles. I'm relieved she welcomes my touch.

After we order the biggest pepperoni pizza on the menu, we find a table outside on the sidewalk. The city noise creates a relaxing ambiance. For a moment, I don't even know how to start the conversation, because there's so much I need to say.

We both open our mouths at the same time, then close them.

"Go ahead," I tell her.

"No, you go first," she says.

"I've missed you so damn much." I search her face and watch her lips turn up into a genuine smile. Before she can respond, her phone starts ringing, and she rejects it.

"I've missed you too, Maverick," she admits.

The phone rings again. I glance down and see it's Rachel,

and I'm so annoyed because we have important things to discuss, things that can't wait, unlike her groceries. When the phone rings again, I answer it.

"Olivia's phone."

"Who is this?" she instantly asks.

I don't have time to be friendly right now. "What do you want, Rachel?"

"Maverick?" she asks, shocked.

"Yep. What do you need?"

"I need to speak to Olivia," Rachel demands.

I look at Olivia sitting on the edge of her chair. I put the phone on speaker so Olivia can hear the rest of the conversation.

"Olivia isn't available for the rest of the day. She will not be picking up your groceries or doing whatever else you need her to do. It can wait. You have run her ragged for the past year, and enough is enough. For once, you need to treat her with the respect she deserves and like a human. You need to learn to treat her better than you treat your goddamn dog, Rachel. Learn how to say thank you and please every once in a while. Learn how to be appreciative of everything she does for you. Otherwise, you're going to lose someone who's running your entire fucking life. Now, do you need anything else or are we done here?"

The line is dead silent.

Olivia sits in front of me with wide eyes and her hands covering her mouth, completely stunned.

"Excuse me?" Rachel finally speaks up.

"You heard every word I said. Olivia will see you first thing Monday morning. She's taking the rest of today, Friday, and the weekend off. She's due for some vacation time after traveling, and you'll be perfectly fine without her for a few days," I tell her, imagining her face and how she's probably internally losing her shit. The thought makes me smile.

"Okay then." Her voice is flat with zero emotion.

"Alright. Nice chatting with you." I hang up, not waiting for her to respond.

The color drains from Olivia's face. "I can't believe you did that. I mean, I should've said those words to her ages ago, but I'm probably going to get fired on Monday. I just know it."

Shaking my head, I grab her hands. "Rachel knows her entire life will fall apart without you. She can't afford to fire you. You run the show, not her."

Olivia lets out a breath. "Okay. I just hope you're right, but I trust you." Her eyes meet mine. "Thank you for sticking up for me. I don't think anyone has ever done that for me before."

"Honestly, I should've done it in Dallas, Denver, or Vegas," I admit. "I hated watching her treat you like that, but it was hard to know my place and if I could say something to her. But enough is enough," I tell her. "But now I have you all to myself without any interruptions." I grab her hand and place a soft kiss on her knuckles. "So what would you like to do for the rest of the day?"

"You have a photo shoot," she reminds me as the most glorious pizza I've ever seen is set on our table. It smells delicious and makes my mouth water.

"Actually..." I linger, grabbing a piece of pizza and trying not to moan out how amazing it is when I take a bite.

Olivia laughs between bites. "It's good isn't it?"

"The best fucking pizza I've ever had," I admit. "Also, the shoot isn't until tomorrow. Presley booked it for Friday, but I decided to come a day earlier. I was hoping to see you. I didn't know you'd be at the studio, though."

She sets her pizza down and looks at me. "Presley knows something's going on between us. She knows all the drama. You really can't tell her anything or even give hints. She's like Scooby Doo and picks up on any sort of clues." She chuckles. "But I'm really happy you're here."

"Me too."

After we've finished the entire pizza, we head back to the Prius.

Once we're inside, I hesitate before starting the car. I turn my body and face her.

"Olivia," I say, grabbing her hand. "I didn't just come here for the photo shoot. I came here because I needed to see you. I'm not giving up on us even if you have or believe it's the right thing to do. I know why you stopped responding to my messages, but I haven't been able to stop thinking about you. Texting with you every day made me feel a happiness I didn't know existed. Just getting to be a part of your life somehow, in any way, felt special to me. I know this whole long-distance thing will be difficult, but I want to try because I want to be with you. Those two weeks we spent together have forever been imprinted on my heart. I let you into a piece of my life that I don't share with anyone. You told me things that I'm sure you don't tell others either. There's something between us, and I don't want to let it go. What we have is special, and I'd be dumb to let you slip through my fingers. On the road, I fell in love with you, Olivia. No amount of distance can change that."

"Maverick," she whispers, squeezing her eyes tight before looking at me. "I'm scared."

I move closer to her. "I know. I am too. But I'm more

scared of losing you. Scared that if I don't take a chance, I'll never know what we could've been. Maybe I'm crazy, but I love you, Olivia. I love you so damn much."

She leans forward and greedily kisses me. She doesn't hesitate when she repeats those four words. "I love you too, Maverick. As crazy as it sounds, I already knew I was falling for you before I left LA."

"It's not crazy. Well, maybe a little." I chuckle. "But I don't care. I know what I feel and that what we shared together was real."

"It was real," she confirms. Her tone is low and daunting, which starts to scare me. " I'm sorry. I'm so sorry for what I did."

I can see she's upset. "What do you mean?" I ask.

"For pushing you away, ignoring your messages, trying to pretend we were better off without each other. I thought that if I stopped talking to you, I'd just be able to forget anything ever happened between us. I tried to get on with my life and stupidly thought it would go back to how things were before I met you. But it was impossible. The more I ignored you, the more I thought about you. It hurt so much, but I was afraid of falling for you, Maverick, even though I already had. I'm afraid I'll end up like my mother." Her voice cracks at the end, and I notice she's tearing up, though she somehow holds herself together. "I've never felt this way about anyone before. It's a foreign feeling for me, and I'm afraid when the newness wears off, you'll no longer be interested."

"Olivia." My voice is soft. "I will love you for as long as you'll let me. I promise you that."

"Forever then?" She slightly smiles.

"Yes, sweetheart. Forever." And when I say those words,

they feel so deeply ingrained in my soul that I know what we have is special. No other person has made me feel so alive, not since my dad passed away.

"I want to bring you home with me," she adds, and I don't argue. "But I'm driving us there."

I tilt my head at her, and we switch places. "I like a woman who takes control." A smile touches my lips because it reminds me of our road trip.

As we're heading through downtown Chicago, I roll down the window. It's not my first visit here, but being with Olivia, makes it feel new and exciting. After she parks on the street, she gets out, and I follow her up the stairs. She unlocks the door and steps aside to allow me to enter. Looking around, all I can do is take it all in. I imagine her walking around in her T-shirt with her hair down working and drinking coffee. This place fits her with the small kitchen, cute living room, and big windows that overlook the street. Everything is neat and perfectly in place, which doesn't surprise me.

I turn around and see her staring at me. "What?" I ask with a half-smile.

"I just..." She shakes her head. "I can't believe you're here right now. Feels like I'm dreaming. Am I?"

Within five steps, I close the space between us and barely pinch her arm. "Nope. I'm really here."

Our mouths violently crash together, and we're ravenous for one another. I've thought about this very moment every day since I planned my trip to Chicago. I was worried she'd reject me, push me away, but as her tongue glides across mine, I know it was a useless concern. She fists my T-shirt in her hands, and it's all the approval I need as I undress her. She's so damn greedy, rushing to take off her clothes, but I stop her.

"I don't want to rush," I admit.

Her eyebrows shoot up. "You pop up out of the blue, and now you want to take it slow?"

I smile with a laugh. "Yeah?"

She lets out a humph and grabs my hand, leading me to her bedroom. "How was the drive? Did you get into any bad weather?"

I chuckle, brushing the hair from her shoulder, kissing the softness of her neck. "It was quick."

"Quick?" She pulls back, slightly confused.

When she looks up at me, I tuck loose hairs behind her ear and dip down to paint my lips across hers. "I flew here."

Her mouth falls open, and I give her a side grin. Shocking her is way too pleasing.

"Wait. You flew? Like on a plane?" Olivia searches my face as if she's waiting for me to say I'm joking.

I chuckle, then nod. "I'd fly to the end of the Earth if that means being with you, Olivia. It was time I faced my fears — all of them."

"Oh my God. I can't believe you flew. I feel awful for ignoring you. I thought I was protecting you from a broken heart. I never imagined you'd come out here," she says.

"I love you, Olivia. I couldn't wait two days to see you, so I booked a flight. The only thing that kept me sane on that plane was the thought of you, the thought of us, together. You were the light at the end of the tunnel."

She pulls me close, holding me in her arms, and smiles. "Thank you for coming here. I missed you more than you'll ever know." She wraps her arms around my neck. Olivia kisses me so passionately, she steals my breath away.

"Baby, I'll do anything to make this work. Long-distance,

texting, FaceTime, phone calls. Weekend flights. I'm not giving up on us."

"Me either. I'm all in," she confirms, and it makes me the happiest man in the world to hear those words.

We make love until the early morning, losing track of time, and only stopping to eat dinner. I feel like I'm in a dream state with her, appreciating every inch of her body. Time almost stands still when we lose ourselves together.

Eventually, we fall asleep, holding each other as if we'll never let go, and this time, I know when I wake up, she'll still be here.

Olivia Carpenter is mine.

CHAPTER TWENTY-THREE

OLIVIA

ONE YEAR LATER

AFTER DOING the whole long-distance relationship thing for the past year, I finally took the leap and packed up my life in Chicago to be with Maverick. Being away from him and having to fly back and forth wasn't the easiest task in the world, but we learned to cherish every moment we had together. Though it never felt like enough. We knew that if we really wanted to see where things could go, we had to be together. So we decided to buy a condo and start in a new, fresh place. It's been the scariest, riskiest, and most exciting thing I've ever done. In his typical Maverick fashion, he's surprising me, and I've only been here for twenty-four hours.

"I don't know why you insist on this stupid blindfold." I laugh as Maverick interlocks his fingers with mine and kisses my knuckles.

"It's because I know you'd peek." I can tell he's smiling. "I know it's hard for you, Miss Priss, but have a little patience. We're almost there."

We've been in the back of an Uber for at least thirty minutes. Several months ago, I finally set some boundaries with Rachel, and she realized she no longer had permission to control my life. She decided to join a yoga class where she surprisingly met someone. This caused her to demand more private time, and once Douglas moved in with her, my shackles were officially removed. Rachel — the micromanaging, needy-as-hell author — no longer needed me the way she once did. I was able to do my job from home like I did for Vada when she'd take her writing retreats. Douglas doesn't allow Rachel to do as she pleases, and he freely puts her in her place and calls her out for being rude, which is what she needs. I need to send him an expensive Christmas gift because the man is a saint for dealing with her day in and day out. It just proves that there's someone out there for everyone — even high-maintenance Rachel.

Telling Rachel I was moving was a bittersweet moment. I didn't want to leave her empty-handed, so I trained a new assistant before I left. I still plan to do administrative duties for her, and we'll do conference calls in between. My goal is to eventually open my own PR and marketing firm. Maverick's career has taken off significantly, and I plan to help him keep up with all of it as well. I'm so excited about this new journey and this next chapter in our lives.

I've never been this happy before, but I know it's because of Maverick more than anything. He's supportive and sweet and everything I need. I squeeze his hand three times, and he leans over and steals a kiss.

The car finally rolls to a stop, and the door cracks open. Maverick gently guides me out. The cool breeze brushes against my cheeks, and I smile.

"The anticipation is almost too much," I tell him as we walk for a little while, then stop.

I feel his body move behind me, and his hands fiddle with the material. Before he undoes the blindfold, he leans in and pulls my earlobe between his teeth. "Ready?"

I keep my eyes closed and pop them open quickly. I gasp as I notice we're standing in a hangar with a plane. I turn and look at Maverick, and he's grinning ear to ear.

"What are we doing?" I ask, somewhat confused.

He twirls a set of keys around his pointer finger. "Going for a ride."

My eyes go so wide they might fall out of the sockets. I look around and realize the car is long gone, and it's just us standing around. "In that? Is that the plane from the photo on your mantel?" I ask, pointing. That picture of them all together and happy is ingrained in my mind.

He nods. "Yeah. It was my dad's private plane, and I found out recently that my mom never sold it. She said she couldn't bring herself to do it, even after all these years, but we thought she had. Instead, she rented it out and stuff to keep it up. Anyway, I had trained when I was younger to be a pilot but never finished getting my license. After doing some research, I realized it wouldn't take much to get certified. So...I did. My dad would be so fucking proud." He's smiling so big that it causes me to smile too.

"Maverick, this is a huge deal." I'm shocked and proud. A tad speechless too.

He shrugs me off and smirks. "I was going to tell you sooner, but I thought it would be more fun to shock the shit out of you. It was worth it."

My jaw is practically on the pavement as he walks to the plane and pulls it out of the hangar.

"Is this real life?" I ask as I follow him around like I'm his shadow as he checks the outside of the plane.

He pulls me into his arms. "Better believe it, baby."

Maverick opens the door and climbs in, then leans over and holds his hand out for me. I follow his lead and step on the wing then sit in the passenger seat. There are so many dials and knobs that I'm completely overwhelmed. He hands me a headset and tells me to put it on, and he puts one on too. We fasten the seat belts, and my heart is pounding so hard in my chest that I swear Maverick can hear it.

"Do you trust me?" he asks.

"Yes, always," I tell him.

"Okay, we're going to do our pre-check. It's required before every flight." I can tell he's being patient with me, probably because I'm nervous as hell.

He reads the list of things out loud and makes sure everything is done before starting the engine. When he turns the key, the propeller comes to life, creating a hum. I look over at him with his headset on as he uses pilot lingo to talk to the tower. My heart is so full right now, I feel like it might burst. This is huge, following in his dad's footsteps after everything that happened, but I get it. It's a way for him to be close to his father in a different way while also facing his fears.

He glances at me and does this cute little scrunchy thing with his nose that's so fucking adorable. I'm listening to Maverick talk back and forth with someone, and it doesn't seem like English other than being cleared for takeoff. I suck in a deep breath and feel my body go tense. I've never been in a plane so small before.

Maverick looks over at me and grabs my hand. "The weather is perfect for flying. It's going to be like glass up there, smooth as can be."

I nod as he positions the aircraft on the runway. Soon we're speeding down it until the plane lifts off the cement and we're in the air soaring above the ground. Looking down, I see a golf course and then the beach.

"Right there is the Santa Monica Pier," Maverick says, pointing as we fly over it. Specks of people are below us, and I can make out the Ferris wheel, roller coasters, and restaurants.

"Wow," I whisper as he turns the plane, and we head toward LA. In the distance, I can see the tall buildings and highways. It's almost unrecognizable from above. Sure, I've flown into LA a dozen times in the past year, but this is more intimate, closer. Once we've been in the air for an hour, I turn and look at Maverick, and he's smiling.

"Okay, where are we going?" I finally ask.

"Thought we'd go on a sky trip." He shoots me a wink.

I smirk. "Do we have enough gas?"

"We better," he adds. "There's no roadside assistance in the sky that's going to deliver us any."

The thought of being stranded in Texas comes to mind. Actually, the whole road trip does. I'm mesmerized by looking out the window, and eventually, Maverick circles around, and we land on another runway. After the wheels touch ground and the plane comes to a complete stop, I'm so ready to straddle his lap and take him.

"Whoa girl," he says between kisses after he turns off the engine.

I giggle. "Pilots are hot."

"If that's all it took…" He trails off, and I need him like I need air. My fingers brush through his hair, and it's hot in the cabin because there's no air conditioner like in a car. By the time we pull away, my lips are throbbing, and his are swollen. Eventually, we climb out of the plane and walk toward a building in the distance. Looking around, I notice we're surrounded by desert. Texas, maybe? Lower Colorado? I try to put the pieces together, but I'm falling short.

After we go inside, Maverick checks in and grabs some keys to a rental car, and we walk out and get inside.

"You've thought about everything, haven't you?" I smile, buckling my seat belt.

"You're just mad because you didn't plan it all," he playfully throws back.

A chuckle escapes me. "You're right. I need to sit back and enjoy it."

As he places the car into drive, he turns on the radio and glances over at me.

"I wasn't going to say anything!" I protest.

"My radio," he reminds me, blasting out Aerosmith.

I look around for anything familiar so I can figure out where we are, and that's when I see the Las Vegas sign. My mouth falls open for the hundredth time today. "Vegas?"

"What gave it away?" He glances over at me with a grin.

"Ha, don't be a smartass," I tell him as we head toward the Strip. When we make it to our hotel, Maverick gets out and hands the keys over to the valet, then goes to the front desk and checks us in. I stand back and wait, and that's when it clicks that we're staying the night. Just as I open my mouth to ask about clothes and everything else, I realize that I'm micromanaging this trip. As he walks up, he notices the color drain from my face and tilts his head at me.

"What's wrong?" he asks as he wraps his arm around my shoulder and we walk toward the elevator.

"I think Rachel has rubbed off on me," I say, which causes him to erupt into a big, hearty laugh.

"That would never happen. You're too compassionate and caring. Pretty sure she sold her soul to the devil in exchange for selling millions of copies of her books."

Now *that* makes *me* laugh.

"I realized I was going to ask you a slew of other questions. So, for the rest of the night or weekend or however long we'll be here, I solemnly swear not to ask about anything else. You're in control," I say just as the elevator comes to a stop at the top floor.

"I kinda like the way that sounds. Me being in control. No questions asked." Maverick unlocks the door, and when I step in, I cover my mouth. The room is bigger than my apartment was in Chicago and even has a fucking chandelier. Champagne is in a bucket, rose petals are sprinkled across the floor, and chocolate-covered strawberries are next to the bed. There's even a suitcase with clothes. He really has thought of everything.

When I turn back around to face him, he's down on one knee with a little black box open.

"Olivia," he says, clearing his throat. I can tell he's nervous by the way his hand is shaking, and I take steps forward to close the space between us. Maverick swallows hard before he continues, but when I look into his eyes, I know exactly what he feels because I feel it too. As much as I didn't want to admit it, I have since the first time I met him.

"You are my sunrise and my sunset. The dust jacket to my favorite book, the send button on an important email, and the caffeine to my coffee," he says, chuckling. "On a serious note, I once told you that I didn't know why I'm still here or what my purpose was in life after losing my dad. After I met you, I knew it was to protect, to care, and to love you. For years, I didn't know what living was truly like and then we went on that road trip, and it changed my life. *You* changed my life, Olivia. Love was like a dream, and something everyone else experienced. Something that only happened in books or movies. I never thought I'd find it, but I fell so madly in love with you that my head is actually still spinning. I can never get enough of you, and any time we've been apart, it's like I'm missing my other half, and I'm so glad I don't have to anymore. Being able to kiss you good night and have you in my arms every morning is a dream come true. You've already made me the happiest man in the world by just giving me a chance and having faith in us. I don't ever want that to end. I want to spend the rest of my life making you laugh and loving you. I know we just made a huge step in our relationship, but I want it all, Olivia. My life is nothing without you. So, Miss Priss, will you marry me?"

I topple him over, kissing him as happy tears stream down my face. I can't be close enough to him, and at this moment, nothing else in the entire world matters. It's like we're the only two people on the planet, and time stands still. My tongue grazes against his, and soon I'm straddling him. All I know is I need him, and I need him right now.

"So," he draws out, laughing and reaching for the box he dropped because we got so caught up in the moment.

"Yes, yes, of course." He slips the gigantic diamond on my finger, and I look at it sparkling in the light. "But... there's one condition," I add with a sly smile.

Maverick searches my face, waiting for my next words.

"Let's get married here. *Today.* You said you didn't want to wait. I don't either." I lean forward and kiss him as his thumbs dig into my hips. He's hard as a rock, and I can feel him through his jeans. "I don't have any family who'd attend anyway. There's really only you and some friends, and I wouldn't be surprised if there's a running bet on when we'll get married."

He laughs, holding his palm to my face. "If I could've married you last year, I would've."

Butterflies swarm in my body. "I've never wanted anything more than to be with you, Maverick. You're my everything. My best friend. My lover. My family. You've seen me at my best and worst. I can't imagine my life without you."

Maverick sits up, pulling me into his arms, and we hold each other for a moment. "Okay. Let's do it. But we're going right now."

I let out a laugh. "I'm calling your bluff."

"There's no bluff, sweetheart. When I make love to you next, you'll be my wife." His lips softly touch mine, and soon we're both on our feet — standing.

My face hurts from the smile that's permanently there. Maverick grabs his phone and does a quick Google search, and after ten minutes, we're using walking directions to one of the dozens of drive-by wedding chapels in Vegas. Nothing has ever felt so right in my life.

As we walk up to the little chapel, I thought I'd feel nervous, but instead, my heart, body, and soul are happy and content, knowing this is how it was always supposed to be. Me and Him. Together forever. He glances over me as if to ask if this is what I want to do, and I don't hesitate before I pull him inside.

After some paperwork is signed, I'm changed into a white wedding dress, and Maverick is fitted into a tux. They even had rings for sale, so then I could slip one onto Maverick's finger until we can go shopping. Strangers are brought in from the street to watch and celebrate. The woman up front gives me quick instructions, which I take like a pro, considering, and soon the "Wedding March" is playing.

As Maverick stands in the front of the room, it's like everything else around us disappears, and I practically glide toward him. An Elvis impersonator comes out and gives us all the cheesy lines until we're pronounced man and wife. The kiss leaves me breathless, and it's as if our hearts permanently meld together at that very moment.

The crowd cheers, and we're quickly moved to a photo area where hurried snapshots are taken of us so we can remember this forever. But the truth is, my heart will never forget.

Soon we're changed from our faux wedding gear into our street clothes and are walking out. I stop and look up at the little chapel, down at the paper in my hand, and then at Maverick.

"I love you." I stand on my tiptoes and paint kisses across his lips.

"I love you, too. Now it's time to consummate our marriage," he adds with a wink, picking me up and carrying me down the sidewalk for at least three blocks. People who pass us don't give us a second glance because we're in Vegas, and weirder things are happening. When we make it back to the hotel and step onto the elevator, I'm practically bursting with happiness.

"We really did it," I say, glancing down at my ring, then at him.

He pulls me into his arms and swipes a piece of hair out of my face. "It's official now, Mrs. Kingston. *I've got you, babe.*"

That damn karaoke song comes to mind, along with all

the special moments we've shared. I nod my head, not taking a moment for granted, realizing how lucky I am to have someone love me and to feel the same way.

"You're right," I tell him with a smirk. "And I've got you, too. Forever."

EPILOGUE

MAVERICK

"OLIVIA! WE'VE GOT TO GO," I shout at her for the third time. So much for my schedule-enforcer wife staying on time.

"I had to pee! Stop shouting," she scolds as she waddles down the hallway.

"Again? Didn't you just go?" I chuckle, knowing she's going to glare at me.

"It's not my fault! Your child is using my bladder as a trampoline," she says, groaning.

I bend down and rub her belly. "It's okay, baby girl. Your mama and I still love you." Looking up, I give Olivia a wink, then kiss her bump. Standing, I cup her face and kiss her softly. "She'll be here before we know it."

"Only ten more weeks," she says excitedly.

"Which is why we need this little babymoon getaway." I smile and press a kiss to her forehead. "You've been working nonstop, and I need some alone time with my wife," I add.

"If only you'd tell me where we're going." She lifts a brow, annoyed that I want to surprise her.

"Not a chance."

I'm so damn proud of her, but she works herself until she's falling asleep at her keyboard, and I have to carry her to bed. A few months after she moved here and we got married, she got serious about starting her own PR and marketing firm. She was able to walk away from Rachel once her replacement was completely trained, and while she helped me with my career, it was time for her to finally do something she was passionate about. I knew how much she loved her job before—even on the bad days—and watching her do something that excites her and has her bouncing on her feet every morning has been worth it. I love seeing her determination and hard work pay off.

I take her hand and lead her to the car. Our bags are already in the back, and although she's begged me to tell her where we're going, I won't budge.

"We're flying?" She gasps when I pull into the airport.

"I told you we were going on a vacation, didn't I?" I look over at her and grin. I've taken her on several trips since I got my license, but I'm most excited about this one because it's a surprise she won't be expecting at all.

Once we're in the air, I look over at my beautiful wife with her growing belly and feel so blessed that our lives have led us here. Never in my wildest dreams would I have imagined a road trip two years ago would bring me the most amazing woman I've ever met. Spending that year flying back and forth was hard, but it's safe to say we definitely made up for it during our first year of marriage.

Hours pass and Olivia falls asleep shortly before we land. I can't wait for her to see where we are. It's gorgeous here, especially in summer. I haven't been to the Carolinas in years.

"We're landing, baby," I tell her through the headset.

"Where are we?" She looks around for clues. "It's so green and beautiful."

"You'll find out in just a minute." I smile, feeling anxious and excited.

Once we're on the ground and the plane is parked, I grab our bags and help Olivia off the plane. She's looking around, trying to put the pieces together, but it's not until she sees Vada standing in the hangar that she realizes exactly where we are.

"No way! Oh my God!" Olivia squeals as Vada runs and nearly lunges at her. She pulls back and hugs her again.

"You look adorable!" Vada gushes.

"I can't believe this!" Olivia turns and faces me. "You brought me to Vada?"

"I know how much you've missed her and figured we could babymoon on the beach."

Olivia closes the gap between us and wraps her arms around my neck as best as she can with her bump in the way. "Thank you. I can't even express how much this means to me."

"It's nice to finally meet you, officially," I say, holding my hand out to Vada. Instead, she pushes it away and gives me a big hug.

"I'm a Southerner now, and in the South, we hug," she explains playfully.

"Where's Ethan and London?" Olivia asks as we walk to Vada's car.

"Waiting for you at the house. They're so excited!"

The surprises aren't over, but I don't tell her that just yet.

Vada drives us to her house where I meet her husband, Ethan, and their son, London. They give us the tour of their house and property, which is pretty awesome. I love the cozy and modern feel to it.

"I can't believe you have a rooster," I say, trying to get the guy to eat food out of my palm.

"That's Henry, and he's an asshole," Vada says dramatically.

"You love him," Ethan protests.

"I remember the stories you told me when you first got here," Olivia says, laughing. "I about died."

"Yeah, it's all fun and games until a cock is trying to bite your ankles!"

Olivia snorts, and I love watching them together. I wish we were closer so she could have a friend like Vada nearby, but I know she's slowly been making new friends in LA.

"Maybe we should've bought a condo here instead," I tease.

"I'm afraid there aren't many modeling opportunities here," Vada jokes. "But maybe a summer house?"

"Don't give him any ideas!" Olivia shouts. "He'll be looking in the homes for sale ads before we go to sleep tonight!"

We all laugh at her outburst, but I don't deny how right she is. Though I'm not surprising her with a summer house, I did find us an awesome rental for our vacation.

After Ethan and I drink a few beers and the girls set dinner on the table, we have a nice, relaxing evening together. Their son is a cutie, and I had fun playing with him too. It has me even more excited for our little girl to arrive.

"We should get going, babe. The Airbnb is about twenty minutes from here, and I have another surprise for you there."

"If it's in your pants, you can save it. I've had that

surprise, and it's how I ended up like this," she says, pointing at her big bump.

"You're the one who couldn't fall asleep," I retort.

Ethan and Vada burst out laughing, and Olivia gives me a look that says she's going to pay me back for that one later.

"We better see you guys before you leave," Vada says when our Uber driver arrives.

"You will," I say with a reassuring smile.

"If you hadn't already run to Vegas to marry him, I'd tell you to marry that man. He's pretty awesome," I hear Vada tell Olivia. They both giggle and hug, and I love seeing her like this.

"So I'm dying to know what else you have planned," Olivia says as we make our way to the rental.

I take her hand and kiss her knuckles twice. "You'll see very soon." I flash her a wink, and she doesn't push for more. I know it's hard for her to give up the control sometimes, but I'm actually impressed by how much she's let go lately. She does so much for her clients that I love being able to spoil her anytime I can.

The driver pulls up, and I watch as Olivia's jaw drops. "Oh my God, what did you do?"

Laughing at her silly outburst, I grab her hand and help her out of the car. Once our bags are out, I tip the guy and lead Olivia to the twenty-foot-tall deck that leads to the beach house. It's on stilts and sits right on the edge of a private beach. I can see the waves hitting the sand behind it as the sun is setting.

"Do you like it?"

"Are you kidding me?" She wraps her arms around my waist. "It's a dream!"

I give her the grand tour, and she kisses me in every

single room, thanking me. This getaway was definitely needed for the two of us before the next chapter in our lives begins, which is in less than three months.

"Let's go watch the sunset," I tell her, leading her out to the deck.

We spend the night staring out at the water, and I even talk her into christening the jet bathtub. It's not easy with her belly, but as a man of determination, I made it work.

"So what are we doing today?" she whispers first thing the next morning.

"I thought you were going to let me surprise you..."

"I am. I was just asking!"

I smile and kiss her forehead. "Let's get ready and dressed, and then you can have your surprise."

"Ugh, fine!"

An hour later, I finally manage to get Olivia up and ready while I make sure everything is set to go without a hitch. She has no idea what's about to happen, and I'm living for the fact that she's not able to guess.

"Are you ready?"

"Hold on. I have to pee. Again!"

I stifle a laugh, knowing she can't help it. Though she did just go fifteen minutes ago.

"Okay, I'm ready. This is really what you want me to wear?" She sways her hips and the dress moves back and forth. She's a goddamn a goddess.

"You look gorgeous," I tell her for the third time.

She flashes me a deadpan look. "I look like a beached whale."

I close the gap between us and bring her into my arms. "My gorgeous beached whale."

"Always the charmer." She wrinkles her nose and chuckles.

"You ready?" I press my lips to her neck and feather kisses along her jawline, loving the way she tastes. No matter how many times we make love, it's never enough. She makes me feel insatiable.

"I guess." She laughs. "What are we doing?"

I pull back to give her a smartass answer, but the doorbell rings right on time.

"Who's here?" she asks.

"Go answer it."

She walks to it and opens the door, and the next second she's squealing.

"Presley, oh my God! What you doing here?" Olivia pulls her inside and wraps her arms around her the best she can.

I walk up behind Olivia and greet Presley. "She's here to take our maternity pictures on the beach."

"What?" Olivia looks at me, then turns to Presley. "Really?"

"I knew you wanted them done, and you said it was hard to coordinate with our schedules, so I planned it for you. Presley squeezed us in before her trip to Texas and said she could meet us here."

"Why are you so amazing?" Olivia turns and is nearly in tears as she wraps her arms around my neck. "I can't believe you did all this."

"When are you going to realize I'm the perfect man?" I tease. "That's what you get for pegging me as a playboy."

She laughs. "Ha! You *were* a playboy!"

"Presley, help me out…"

"I'm not getting in the middle of this. You two are sickly adorable, and it makes me want to throw up."

"Oh come on! You'd find the perfect guy, too, if you'd sit still long enough to meet someone," Olivia tells her.

"She is going to Texas next week," I add.

"Ooh! Find yourself a hot cowboy to ride and then tell me all about it," Olivia encourages with eagerness. "Seriously, I expect some juicy details. I've read some cowboy romances, and if there's one thing those cowboys are good at —"

"Okay, I don't need the details." Presley stops her with a laugh. "I'll be staying at a B&B on a ranch. If I meet any real-life cowboys, I'll jump at the opportunity. Happy now?"

"Very." Olivia smiles victoriously.

"You ready to get your pictures done? The view is amazing," Presley says.

"Yes, let's do it!"

The three of us head toward the beach and step in the shallow part of the water. Presley poses us and has us look at each other and facing different directions while she snaps away. Olivia looks so damn happy, I can't wait for her to see these shots.

My hand is over her bump, and I feel a kick against my palm. "I think she's dancing in there," I say, placing both hands over her stomach. "She's having fun." Feeling our baby girl inside her never gets old.

I kneel in front of her, and I can hear Presley taking more snapshots. "I can't wait to meet you, baby." Looking up and seeing my gorgeous wife with her golden hair blowing in the wind and her eyes bright with happiness causes my heart to burst with the love I feel for her and our little one. "Thank you for marrying me."

"What?" she asks softly.

"Seriously. I can't imagine my life without you. Thanks for giving me the chance to prove you wrong."

"Prove me wrong?" She arches a brow.

"That I wasn't a playboy just looking to get into your pants." I wink. "And that you were more than just an uptight, prissy know-it-all."

"That was almost romantic until you ruined it." She grins.

I stand and steal a kiss. "I love you."

"You're lucky I love you too."

He smirks. "So fucking lucky."

NEXT IN THE BEDTIME READS SERIES

Never trust a man who wears nothing more than a cowboy hat and ripped jeans who asks if you'd like to save a horse and ride a . . . well, you get the picture.

That should've been enough for me to walk away.

I've been warned on several occasions about southern men — with their sexy accents, charming manners, and the ability to easily get any woman in bed — which is something I'll be avoiding.

Being a professional photographer has many perks — traveling around the world, calling all the shots, and working with subject matter that isn't bad to look at — but Colton Langston with his washboard abs and baby blue eyes, could care less about my current project. He's trouble, I know it, and he's determined to make me work for every single photo. When I'm forced into riding lessons, I get way more than I ever bargained for, and by the time my trip is over, I'm in too deep.

Being with him was thrilling, but falling for him was unpredictable.

And ignoring him will be impossible.

ABOUT THE AUTHOR

Brooke Cumberland and Lyra Parish are a duo of romance authors who teamed up under the *USA Today* pseudonym, Kennedy Fox. They share a love of *You've Got Mail* and *The Holiday*. When they aren't bonding over romantic comedies, they like to brainstorm new book ideas. One day, they decided to collaborate under a pseudonym and have some fun creating new characters that'll make your lady bits tingle and your heart melt. If you enjoy romance stories with sexy, tattooed alpha males and smart, quirky, independent women, then a Kennedy Fox book is for you! They're looking forward to bringing you many more stories to fall in love with!

CONNECT WITH US

Find us on our website:
kennedyfoxbooks.com

Subscribe to our newsletter:
Kennedyfoxbooks.com/newsletter

Join our reader group:
Facebook.com/groups/kennedyfoxbooks

facebook.com/kennedyfoxbooks

twitter.com/kennedyfoxbooks

instagram.com/kennedyfoxbooks

amazon.com/author/kennedyfoxbooks

goodreads.com/kennedyfox

bookbub.com/authors/kennedy-fox

BOOKS BY KENNEDY FOX

AN ENEMIES-TO-LOVERS DUET
TRAVIS & VIOLA
Checkmate: This is War
Checkmate: This is Love

A FRIENDS-TO-LOVERS DUET
DREW & COURTNEY
Checkmate: This is Reckless
Checkmate: This is Effortless

A SECOND-CHANCE ROMANCE DUET
LOGAN & KAYLA
Checkmate: This is Dangerous
Checkmate: This is Beautiful

BISHOP BROTHERS SERIES
Taming Him
Needing Him
Chasing Him
Keeping Him

BEDTIME READS SERIES
Falling for the Bad Boy
Falling for the Playboy
Falling for the Cowboy

Made in the USA
Columbia, SC
15 December 2018